THE SPRITE SISTERS

THE GHOST IN THE TOWER

SHERIDAN WINN

PICCADILLY PRESS · LONDON

The Sprite Sisters series

The Circle of Power
The Magic Unfolds
The Secret of the Towers
The Ghost in the Tower
New Magic

First published in Great Britain in 2009
by Piccadilly Press Ltd,
5 Castle Road, London NW1 8PR
www.piccadillypress.co.uk

A catalogue record for this book is available
from the British Library.

ISBN: 978 1 84812 029 7 (paperback)

Printed in the UK by CPI Bookmarque, Croydon, CR0 4TD
Cover design by Simon Davis
Cover illustration by Anna Gould
Sprite Towers map by Chris Winn

Mixed Sources
Product group from well-managed
forests and other controlled sources
www.fsc.org Cert no. TT-COC-002227
© 1996 Forest Stewardship Council

FSC

For my son Alex
and my daughter Rosie,
with love

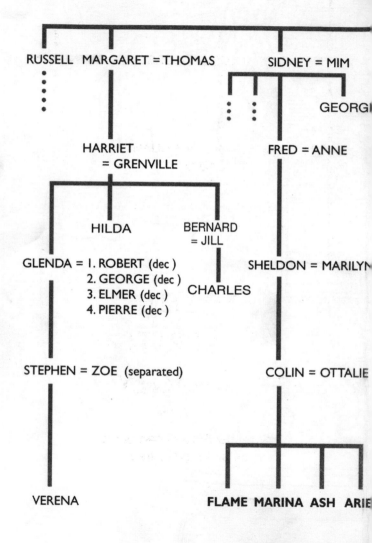

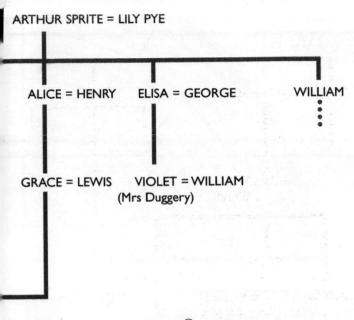

ARTHUR SPRITE = LILY PYE

ALICE = HENRY   ELISA = GEORGE   WILLIAM

GRACE = LEWIS   VIOLET = WILLIAM
(Mrs Duggery)

THE
SPRITE
FAMILY

This is just a small part of the
complete family tree.

THE CIRCLE
OF POWER

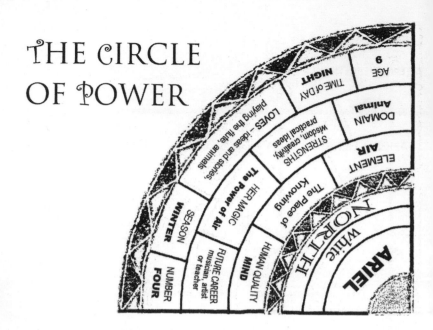

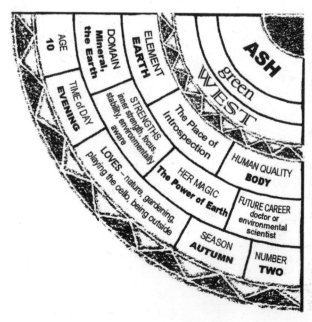

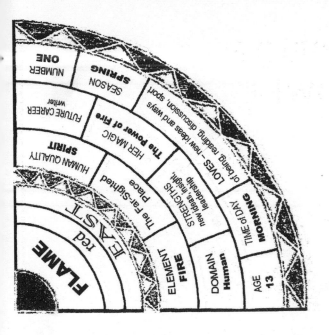

FLAME — red — EAST

NUMBER	ONE
SEASON	SPRING
FUTURE CAREER	writer
HER MAGIC	The Power of Fire
HUMAN QUALITY	SPIRIT
	The Far-Sighted Place
STRENGTHS	new ideas, insight, leadership
LOVES	new ideas and ways of being, reading, discussion, sport
TIME of DAY	MORNING
ELEMENT	FIRE
DOMAIN	Human
AGE	13

MARINA — yellow — SOUTH

NUMBER	THREE
FUTURE CAREER	actress or singer
HUMAN QUALITY	EMOTIONS
	The Place of Feelings
SEASON	SUMMER
HER MAGIC	The Power of Water
ELEMENT	WATER
STRENGTHS	playfulness, trust, empathy
DOMAIN	Plants and trees
LOVES	singing, dancing and acting, talking to friends, sport
TIME of DAY	AFTERNOON
AGE	12

CHAPTER ONE

THE
POWER OF WATER

IT WAS a Sunday morning in late October, the first bright day after weeks of wind and heavy skies. In the gently undulating Norfolk countryside, Sprite Towers glowed in the sunlight. The woods were bright with the autumn hues of caramel, gold, scarlet and amber. Around the huge, red-brick house, fields of newly planted barley and stubble formed a patchwork of colour.

As the Sprites ate their breakfast, things felt tranquil. In the warm kitchen, the smell of bacon, eggs, toast and coffee filled the air.

'I can't believe we'll have a puppy in a few hours' time,' said Ariel, a dreamy look on her face.

Mum smiled at her, then caught Dad's eye. He turned to his daughters and said, 'I hope you're all prepared for some

1

work, because young dogs demand a lot of time and energy.'

'Oh yes, we are,' Flame, Marina, Ash and Ariel chorused.

'What time are we going to see the puppies?' asked Flame.

'Half past two,' replied Dad.

'How big is the litter?' asked Marina.

'Seven, Harry said – four male pups and three female,' replied Dad, munching a piece of toast.

'And which are we having?' asked Flame.

Dad paused, then said, 'Well, there's Bert to think of. We need to have another male with him about. And since almost everyone in this household is female, *I'd* like a boy!'

'What does Bert think?' asked Ash, looking round at the little sausage dog sitting in his basket by the Aga, with his back to them.

'Oh dear – I think he's sulking,' said Marina.

Bert was Grandma's dog. When she came to live at Sprite Towers four years ago, she brought him with her.

'He'll be fine – I'll make a fuss over him,' said Grandma. As if he understood her words, Bert got out of his basket, trotted underneath the big kitchen table and nestled at her feet. Grandma leaned down to stroke his long, silky ears.

'Why have we never had our own dog before?' asked Marina.

Dad shrugged and looked at Mum.

The Sprite Sisters looked at Mum. 'There was enough to do looking after you lot!' she laughed.

'Well, not long to wait now, girls,' said Dad.

When breakfast was cleared up, Mum and Flame put on big white aprons and weighed out flour to begin the week's bread making. Grandma went upstairs to tidy the girls' bedrooms and Ariel cleaned out her gerbils in the utility room. Marina and Ash said they'd clean out the rabbit and guinea pig hutches, down by the stables.

'I'll be out soon, Ash,' said Dad, smiling at his third eldest daughter. 'Just got to make a phone call.'

'Okay, Dad,' Ash smiled back. They spent many happy hours working together in the vegetable garden. 'We must check the pumpkins.'

'Ah yes – Hallowe'en,' chuckled Dad, and off he went to his office.

Marina and Ash pulled on their jumpers and wellies, then raced across the lawn towards the stables.

Marina laughed as she ran beside her sister, enjoying the feel of the cool, clear air on her face. But halfway across the lawn she stopped suddenly and stared down at the grass.

Ash spun round and caught her breath. 'What's the matter?'

Marina was gazing at the ground, a look of concentration on her face. She looked up at her sister and said, 'Something's changed. Can you feel it?'

Ash stood still and placed her palms downwards towards the grass. Then she closed her eyes and focused her mind. Using her magic power of Earth, she tried to feel what was happening. After a few seconds, she looked at Marina and nodded. 'There's something moving in the ground down here.'

'It's water,' said Marina, holding out her hands, palm down. 'There's water under this grass. It's rising up to the surface.'

'Where's it coming from?'

'Deep in the ground.'

Marina looked around the wide rolling lawn. They were standing halfway between the house and the stables. In front of them were the stables, behind them the house and to the right was the Secret Garden.

Ash closed her eyes again and was quiet for a while. She thought about her magic power and how it enabled her to sense what was happening in the ground. In her mind was a clear picture of long, thick tree roots, wiry roots of the lawn grass, tunnels made by moles and knobbly flints that lay deep in the soil.

Ash had the power to bind: if she pointed her finger at an object or a human being, it would not move a millimetre. It would stay stock-still, as if gripped by strong roots, until she removed her power.

Marina's power of Water enabled her to create movement and change in fluids. She could create a river or a flood, suck out the fluid from something or turn it to ice.

Flame's power was Fire. Nothing could escape the heat that emanated from the fingers of the eldest Sprite Sister if she directed her magic power. It would melt or burn in an instant.

Ariel's power of Air balanced her three sisters' magic. She could send things high into the air. Even a human being could be sent spinning when the youngest Sprite pointed her finger at them.

Now Ash gazed down at the earth. 'Yes, I can feel it,' she said, looking round at Marina. 'Something is moving.'

Marina walked up and down. Her mind focused as she visualised the water under the ground. 'There's a lot of water under here,' she said, moving her hand in a big circle. 'It feels like the pressure is increasing.'

Ash looked up at the grass in front of the stables, some thirty feet away, and pointed. 'What's that?'

The sisters ran over the lawn and stopped in front of a puddle of water forming on the grass.

'It looks like water running from a hose – except there is no hose,' said Marina.

'It's bubbling up from the ground,' said Ash, peering down. 'How weird!' She put her fingers in the cool, clear water.

'I *knew* there was water here – I could *feel* it,' said Marina, putting her hand in it, too. 'I wonder if we could drink it?'

'Better wait and see what Dad says,' said Ash. 'I'll go and get him.' As she stood up, the water began to spurt a little higher in the air.

'Hey, look – it's getting stronger,' said Marina. She watched, fascinated, as Ash ran towards the house.

A minute later, Flame, Ariel and Ash charged over the lawn. Mum, Dad and Grandma followed. As the girls arrived, the water suddenly spurted up into a little fountain about half a metre high.

'Whoa!' shouted Ariel, her mouth dropping open in amazement.

Flame walked straight towards the water and held out her hand. 'It's very cold!' she laughed, her eyes wide with excitement.

'Can we drink it, Dad?' asked Ash, as he approached.

Dad's face creased into a big smile. 'Well, I never!' he said, staring at the fountain. 'Probably, Ash – but we'd better get it tested first.'

'Where's it coming from, Dad?' asked Ariel.

'It's probably an aquifer – an underground spring,' he replied. 'This whole area has chalk under the ground. Chalk is porous, so water can move through it. The water can't move through the rock deep under the ground, so when the pressure builds it moves up through the chalk. Then it breaks out – and I think that's what has happened here. We're at the highest point around, which is where the water will come out.'

'Colin, if it's an aquifer could we sink in a borehole?' asked Mum. 'It would be nice to have our own water supply.'

'Especially if it's good for drinking,' he agreed.

'Yes, lovely fresh water – and we'd save on our water bills,' said Mum.

'What's a borehole?' asked Ash.

'It's like a well,' replied Dad. 'It's a way of getting the water out of the ground. You drill a hole in the ground and seal it off. Then you sink a pipe and put in a pump to take the water to the house.'

'Why don't you ask Harry to come over and dowse for it?' suggested Mum.

'Good idea,' said Dad. He took out his phone and rang their friend and neighbour, who lived on the big farm next to Sprite Towers.

'What's dowsing?' asked Ariel.

'It's a way of finding things like water channels under the ground,' said Mum. 'Harry can do it. It looks like magic – you'll see.'

The Sprite Sisters smiled at one another, then at their grand-mother. Their parents had no idea about their daughters' magic powers, so Marina and Ash could not tell them they had already worked out that there was a lot of water under the lawn. Grandma knew all about their powers, however. Long ago, she had had the magic power that ran through the Sprite family. She smiled at Marina as if to say, 'I expect you already know all about it.'

Ten minutes later, Harry arrived in his muddy Land Rover. The big, cheery farmer strode over the lawn towards them, clutching two L-shaped brass rods. 'So what have you got here then, eh?' he smiled. With him was his black Labrador, Teasel.

'Morning, Harry – thanks for coming over so quickly,' said Dad.

'You're welcome,' replied Harry. 'That's quite a fountain! Must be a significant pressure of water under there. And you say it appeared this morning?'

'About half an hour ago,' said Marina. 'Ash and I were walking over the lawn. It started as a little pool of water on the grass, then it suddenly got stronger. Will it flood out the rabbits and guinea pigs over there?'

Harry looked at the hutches in the stable yard. 'No. Most of the water will just drain back into the ground.' He bent down, held out one of his huge hands and caught some of the water. Beside him, Teasel lapped it up.

'Tastes good,' said Harry, drinking from his hand. 'Looks like you've got an aquifer under here, Colin. Should be able to drill a borehole.'

'That's what I thought,' said Dad.

'Right, let's have a dowse,' said Harry. They all watched as he held out the two L-shaped brass rods in front of him.

Marina was tempted to step forward and say, 'It's okay, everyone, I've already worked out that there's water under here, using my magic power!' – but she stayed quiet.

Flame grinned at her, knowing what she was thinking.

Harry started to walk slowly around the grass. The Sprite Sisters held their breath, wondering what would happen. Suddenly, the two brass rods began to spin fast in circles moving away from one another. As Harry walked round, they kept spinning.

Ariel's eyes popped open with amazement.

Everybody burst out laughing. Dad put his arm around Ash's shoulder. 'Impressive, eh?' he said.

'Yes,' agreed Ash and wondered what he would say if she showed him her magic powers.

Harry walked in a wide circle around the fountain of water. All the time, the rods spun round in circles, the right one spinning clockwise and the left spinning anti-clockwise. Then he came all the way back to the fountain of water and stopped. 'Feels as if there's quite a bit of water under here,' he said.

'Where do you think they'll drill a borehole?' asked Dad.

'Here, I should say,' replied Harry, pointing at the fountain. 'It tastes clean, so I should say you've got a pure supply. Nice thing to have in your garden.'

What Harry did not know – what none of the Sprites knew, as they stood there looking at the water – was that something else was stirring under the ground. Unseen by them, a dark energy was moving through the soil, carried by the flow of the water.

CHAPTER TWO

AFTER SUNDAY lunch of roast beef and home-grown vegetables, the Sprites got into the big red car and drove to Harry's farm. Ariel was so excited she could not sit still. Mum and Dad talked in the front. Grandma sat behind and looked out of the window.

As they pulled up in front of the big red-brick farmhouse, Dad turned round. The Sprite Sisters stopped chattering.

'Right, girls, let's be clear,' he said. 'I know you'll want to bring the whole litter home, because the puppies will *all* be adorable, but we are getting *one* only. So that we don't have any problems with Bert, it's to be a male puppy. There are four male puppies, so we'll need to choose one of those.'

A few minutes later, Harry and his wife, Charlotte, their

twins, Liam and George, and daughter, Ellie, took the Sprites round the side of the house to one of the stables. Harry opened the big wooden door and they all walked in. At the back of the stable, lying in a basket, was Meg, Harry's other black Labrador and the mother of the puppies. In front of her, the ground was covered with straw – and the straw was covered in little fluffy bundles, only ten weeks old. Before Harry had had time to suggest the Sprites just look at the pups for a little while, each of them had picked up a puppy. Liam and George picked up two more and handed them to Mum and Grandma.

Little Ellie, who was six, picked up the seventh pup and stroked its wet nose.

'Ellie, give him to Mr Sprite to hold!' said Liam. He and his brother were nine and in Ariel's class at school.

Ellie handed the pup to Dad.

'Thank you, Ellie,' he smiled, taking the little round pup from her.

'Look at this tail,' said Flame. 'It's so cute.' And she stroked the tiny spike that would soon grow into a proper tail.

'This one's so soft,' said Marina, putting her face against the puppy's coat.

'Look at his pink stomach,' said Ash, stroking the little round belly of another.

'Puppy heaven,' said Ariel, stroking the tiny wet nose of another small black puppy.

Harry and Charlotte and their children looked on, amused, as the Sprites swapped puppies.

'They're *all* delightful,' said Mum, turning to Harry. 'Goodness knows how we'll decide which one to take.'

Harry smiled. 'If you put them down, we can have a look at them running around.'

'Good idea,' said Mum.

One by one, the Sprites placed the puppies back on the straw.

Then Harry leaned down and picked up the three female pups in his big hands. Then he turned to Mum and beamed. 'That's better,' he said, in his gruff farmer's voice. 'Now you can see the male puppies. Just watch them for a little while. You'll soon get an idea of what they're each like.'

'Okay,' replied Mum.

The Sprites watched the four puppies.

'He's the biggest,' said Dad, pointing to one.

'He's the smallest,' said Marina, pointing to another.

'That one is so cute!' said Ariel, pointing to a third.

The fourth male puppy, the second biggest, ran around for a little while, then sat down on its plump little bottom a few metres away and looked up at the Sprites. It just watched them. It didn't demand attention. It was its own dog.

'*That*'s the one!' Flame, Marina, Ash and Ariel all said at once.

'Yes,' agreed Mum and Dad.

Grandma smiled. 'We always did appreciate a spirit of independence in our family,' she said.

They all laughed, then Harry said, 'Good choice. That's the one I would have picked.'

Mum held the new puppy – to save any arguments – and they all went into the house. There, Charlotte gave Mum a sheet of paper with the feeding instructions for the next few months and details of the inoculations the pup would need.

'You mustn't take him outside until he's had his jabs,' said Harry. 'You can carry him outside, but don't put him down on the ground.'

'He'll probably cry for the first few nights, as he's not used to being alone,' said Charlotte. 'But you must leave him. He'll soon adapt.'

'Bert will keep him company,' said Grandma.

The Sprites got into the big red car and drove back to Sprite Towers. As they made their way along the country lanes, the pup lay on Mum's lap with a look of contentment on his tiny, fluffy face.

Immediately, names were suggested. 'Wellington,' said Dad, as he clutched the steering wheel.

'Wellington?' shouted the Sprite Sisters. 'We can't call him *that*!'

'Why not?' retorted Dad.

'He'll sound like a boot!' giggled Ariel.

'I'll have you know that Wellington was a very famous man,' said Dad, piqued.

Mum grinned.

'All right, what about Winston – as in Churchill?' said Dad. 'Good solid name – and another famous Englishman.'

'No, Dad!' the Sprite Sisters groaned.

'He sounds middle-aged already,' said Flame.

'So what are your ideas, then?' said Dad, bristling.

'Fizzy!' shouted Ariel from the back.

'*Fizzy?*' said Dad, aghast.

'No, Ariel,' said Flame. 'That's what you'd call a guinea pig.'

'Humph,' said Ariel, pushing her ski-jump nose in the air.

When they got home, the puppy was placed in his basket by the Aga. Immediately, he clambered out and knocked his food and water bowls all over the floor.

Then he was introduced to Bert.

If Bert had eyebrows, he would have raised one of them. I'm the boss, he seemed to say. The little puppy watched, as Bert sat, majestically, eyeing him. Then Bert got up, walked round the little dog and sniffed him. With that, the puppy licked him, happily, then bumbled off and knocked over the water bowl once more. Every few seconds, one of the Sprite Sisters tried to pick him up, until Mum insisted they just let him get his bearings.

'He's *so* sweet,' drooled Marina.

'This is blissful,' sighed Ariel.

After a while, Mum said, 'I think we'd better let him rest now – he must be worn out.'

'I ought to go down and see what's happening to the water on the lawn,' said Dad, and he went off to get his boots.

'We'll come too,' said Mum.

'Can I carry the pup, Mum?' asked Flame. 'We can't leave him here alone just yet.'

'Okay, love,' she agreed. 'But don't put him down.' Then she said, 'Put on your boots, girls. It's wet on the lawn.'

A minute later, the Sprite family followed Dad over the grass. He walked quickly with his long strides. Bert lolloped along beside Grandma. Flame carried the puppy.

'The fountain's dropped a little,' said Marina, as they got closer.

'The pressure must have decreased,' said Dad.

'The grass is soaking,' said Ariel. 'Look, the water is all the way over there.' And she ran off, sploshing her feet in the water.

'It's like a huge puddle,' said Flame.

'How far does the water go, Dad?' asked Ash.

'Under the whole garden, as we're on the top of the hill.'

'What happens if it doesn't stop?' asked Ash.

'More springs would break out around the hill, to release the pressure,' said Dad, looking around the lawn. 'There's a surprisingly large amount. I'll call the engineers in the morning.'

Ash wasn't listening; she was lost in thought. She'd had the sudden feeling that there was something else under the grass, apart from water – and it wasn't a nice feeling.

Flame noticed. 'What's up?' she asked her sister, quietly.

'There's something odd here,' said Ash.

'Underneath the grass?'

Ash nodded and stared down.

'What sort of odd?' asked Flame.

'Don't know,' said Ash, shaking her head. 'It's as if – as if something is trapped under here.'

Just then Mum called, 'Okay, girls, come on, you've got music practice to do before supper and we must get this puppy settled in.'

'And choose a name,' said Marina, linking her arm in her mother's as they turned to walk back to the house.

'Yes, that could take some time,' said Mum.

'Why?' asked Ariel, bouncing up.

'Because we've all got our own ideas, silly, that's why!' said Marina. And she let go of her mother's arm and raced her sister back over the lawn to the house.

* * *

The 'Naming of the New Puppy' conversation began in earnest at the supper table. By that time, the little dog had been fed twice, cuddled umpteen times and placed back in its new basket. Now he was fast asleep. Bert looked on, his sharp nose pointed in the air, as if he didn't approve of all the fuss.

'I still like Wellington,' said Dad.

'No, Dad, no!' the Sprites Sisters groaned.

'Okay, let's have some ideas then,' he said.

'Mango,' said Ash.

'Hm,' said Dad.

'Tosh,' said Flame.

'I quite like Tosh,' said Mum.

'Harry,' suggested Grandma.

'Smarties,' said Ariel.

'Rollo,' said Grandma.

'Berry,' suggested Mum.

'Reg,' suggested Flame, grinning.

'Yeah, right,' said Marina, screwing up her face.

'It's got to be something you can call easily,' said Mum.

'Okay, let's go for a name with one or two syllables,' said Dad.

'Wellington's got three – so we can't have that,' said Flame.

Dad smiled. 'Graham,' he said, a twinkle in his eye.

'Oh Gawd, Dad, that's *awful*! You can't call a dog "Graham"!' said Flame, stabbing a piece of tomato.

'Mungo,' suggested Ash.

'Raisin,' suggested Marina.

'Brandy,' ventured Flame.

'Pickle,' said Ariel.

'No, that's another guinea pig name,' said Marina.

'Snotburger, then,' said Ariel.

'*Ariel Sprite!*' said Mum, aghast. Flame, Marina and Ash laughed.

Ariel giggled. 'Thought you'd like that one, Mum.'

'We are absolutely not calling any pets *Snotburger*,' said Mum.

'Anyway, it's three syllables,' grinned Flame.

'Winston – that's two syllables,' said Dad, miles away.

They all munched silently for a moment. Then Dad said, 'It's got to be something strong and straightforward. Not a *diddly* sort of name. I mean, he looks sweet and cuddly at the moment, but our puppy will soon grow into a big dog with a deep bark. He needs a strong, simple name.'

They were silent again, each thinking hard. Then Grandma said, 'What about Archie? I've always liked that name – and it means "true and bold".'

Everyone looked at her. Dad nodded. 'Hm,' he said. 'Good name.'

Mum nodded. 'I like it, Marilyn.'

The Sprite Sisters all nodded.

'He *looks* like an Archie,' said Flame.

'It's a nice name,' agreed Marina.

'"True and bold" is perfect,' said Ash.

Ariel nodded, while chewing on a large mouthful of salad.

'Okay, hands up all those in favour of calling our new puppy "Archie",' said Dad.

Everyone raised their hands. Dad smiled at Grandma.

'Well, Ma, seems you've carried the day.'

'Archie it is then!' she laughed.

'Thank heavens we've found a name we all like,' said Dad. 'I thought we'd be debating this till Christmas.'

He looked over at Archie, who was asleep in his basket, worn out by the day's activities.

'Winston!' called Dad across the kitchen. The puppy slept on.

'Mungo!' called Dad. No response.

'Smarties,' he called again. Nothing.

Then he called, 'Archie!' The little pup raised his head and sat up. He looked over at Dad, as if to say, 'Are you talking to me?'

The Sprites burst out laughing.

After supper, Dad grabbed his boots and said, 'I'm just going out to check that water.'

Marina and Ash grabbed theirs, too. 'We'll come with you,' they said.

While Dad mooched about on the lawn pointing his torch, Ash whispered to Marina, 'What do you think?'

'There's more water,' replied Marina, looking round.

For a moment they were silent. Then Ash said, quietly, 'It feels to me as if the earth is being disturbed – as if there's some other force moving here, apart from the water.'

Marina nodded. 'Yes – I can feel something running through the water.'

'It's very strange,' said Ash. 'I wonder what's going on?'

CHAPTER THREE

THE GHOST AWAKENS

ASH WAS right. There was something stirring under the ground at Sprite Towers – and it wasn't just the water. A restless, malevolent energy was beginning to make its way out of the earth, flowing upwards with the water.

It was the second time in a matter of months that Sprite Towers had been assailed by water and dark forces. At the end of June, in a wet summer, the Sprite Sisters' vengeful enemy, Glenda Glass, had tried to buy the house and throw out the Sprites. She had used her dark power to weaken the roof, so that it would collapse. Water had gushed down the walls and the timbers had rotted. Such would be the cost of repairing the immense expanse of timber and tile, that the Sprites would have been forced to sell. There had been a huge battle between the Sprite Sisters and Glenda Glass, which the girls had won. Peace had been restored and the house was safe.

Now something was about to attack Sprite Towers from below.

When the girls got home from school on Monday, Flame, Marina and Ariel played with Archie, while Ash went outside to see what was happening. Her father joined her and they walked together over the lawn in the gathering twilight.

'The engineers are coming tomorrow morning,' said Dad.

'That's good,' said Ash. 'Look, the fountain's subsided a bit more.'

'The pressure has diminished,' said Dad, holding up the torch. 'But there's still a lot of water coming out. Surprising, that it's happened so suddenly!' Then he added, 'What is it with Sprite Towers and water, eh? We've had the leaking roof, now we've got a flood on the lawn.'

Ash felt uneasy. There was definitely something wrong, she thought. For a moment, she closed her eyes and used her magic power of Earth to feel what was happening. It's as if something's trying to get out of the earth, she thought. A cold, cold feeling struck her in the heart. Ash shuddered.

Her thoughts were interrupted as Dad motioned the torch towards the vegetable garden. 'Let's go and have a quick look at the pumpkins while we're here,' he said.

'Okay,' said Ash, and they walked through the huge beech hedge into the vegetable garden. Nestled in the far corner underneath the high brick wall was the pumpkin bed.

Dad shone the torch. An array of orange pumpkins gleamed in the beam of light. 'They're looking good,' he said. 'You'll have some fun scooping those out for Hallowe'en.'

'And we'll be eating pumpkin soup till Christmas,' laughed Ash.

As they walked back over the lawn, Ash asked, 'Dad, has anyone ever dug up the lawn? Do you know if there's anything underneath it?'

'Well, there was another house here, before Sprite Towers was built,' said Dad. 'I believe it was around here on the lawn. There may be bits of the foundations still there – the cellar, most likely, as that would have lain underground.'

'What sort of house was it?'

'A very old house. I think Sidney Sprite's sister lived there. Ask Grandma – she'll be sure to know.'

And with that they went back in.

In the kitchen, Flame, Marina and Ariel were playing with Archie. As Dad and Ash walked in, the little puppy got so excited that he peed on Dad's foot.

The girls all burst out laughing. Dad looked less than enthusiastic and cleaned it off with some kitchen roll. 'Terrific,' he said.

'Don't worry, it's not just you – Archie's been making puddles everywhere,' said Mum. 'I seem to have been mopping up all day.'

By the time Ash came back in Grandma had left to go to supper with some friends, so she didn't have a chance to ask her about the old house. Later, as the girls cleaned their teeth,

Ash told her sisters what Dad had said. They were intrigued.

'We must find out,' said Flame. 'I wonder why nobody has ever mentioned it before.'

'Dad's so vague about stuff like that – he probably didn't even think about it,' said Marina.

'Well, we must ask Grandma,' said Flame. However, in the morning, as they dashed to get ready for school, there wasn't time to talk to her then either – not without Mum there. So they went off to school, still not knowing anything much about the house under the garden.

Ash pondered over this question as she walked about the school between lessons. Flame Sprite had other things on her mind. The question of who would be chosen as captain for the girls under-14 hockey team was at the forefront of her thoughts. Would the hockey coach choose her – or would she choose Verena Glass?

Glenda Glass's granddaughter was equally keen to be chosen and as good a hockey player as Flame. Both girls were fast, strategic in their play and very determined. They even looked similar: tall, with long, straight hair – although where Verena was blond, Flame's hair was a deep copper. They both had the glint of competition in their eyes. Neither liked to be beaten – but only one would be chosen as captain.

So Flame kept away from Verena, her distant Sprite cousin, that day. As she walked across the Quad at Drysdale's School that morning, she pictured magnets pushing apart – like her science teacher had demonstrated in physics. Verena and I are like magnetic opposites, thought Flame. We're of equal force and we always push each other away.

Marina Sprite, on the other hand, was drawn to Verena Glass. Despite Marina being over a year younger, the two girls had become friends. An only child living with a cold and seemingly heartless grandmother, Verena appreciated Marina's warm, empathetic nature. So it was natural that, when they met in the Quad after lunch, they chatted.

'What's up?' asked Marina, detecting a look of sadness on Verena's face.

'I've had an email from my mother. She wants to come home.'

'But that's wonderful!' said Marina. 'Aren't you pleased?'

'Yes, of course,' sighed Verena. 'I hate living with Grandma, and I never really understood why Mummy went off to South America and just left us.'

Marina waited, silent, as Verena thought about this for a few seconds.

Verena looked into Marina's kind eyes and said, quietly, 'She's written to me to say that she's made a dreadful mistake going off with this other man – and that she still loves Daddy. She wants to come home.'

'Does your father know?'

Verena shook her head. 'I don't know. He may do – though I sort of had this feeling she was sounding me out. You know, like fishing for information.'

'What's stopping her coming back?'

'Well, if she wants to come home here she needs to know if Daddy still wants her back. He was pretty angry that she left. And how would she live at The Oaks with Grandma? You know I get this feeling that Grandma doesn't like

Mummy, that she wants her out of the way.'

'Does your father know you're unhappy with your grandmother?'

'I never say much,' said Verena. 'I doubt he'd believe me. She's his mother – and she's so different with him. He doesn't see her as I see her.'

And I bet he doesn't have a clue about Glenda's dark magic powers, thought Marina. Nobody would believe that – except us Sprite Sisters and Grandma. We know how evil she can be.

'So what are you going to do?' asked Marina.

'I don't know. Tell Daddy, I suppose.'

'Yes – I think you should. Will you tell your grandmother?'

Verena looked down and she shook her head. 'No, I don't tell her anything. We hardly speak at home.'

Marina put her arm around Verena's shoulders. 'Why don't you talk to our mum about it?' she suggested. 'You know how well you and she get on. She's a good listener – and she's really good at solving problems.'

'Do you think she would talk to me?' A look of hope spread across Verena's face.

'Yes,' Marina smiled. 'She'd be worried if she knew how you are feeling. She always says it concerns her that your mother is so far away.'

'How would I speak to her?'

'Cycle round at the weekend – tell your grandmother you're coming over to see us. I'll tell Mum that you might come over.'

'Thanks, Marina,' said Verena. 'I really appreciate that.'

They were silent for a moment, then Verena said, 'You know, it's a funny thing being pretty and coming top in everything and winning all the time. I've found I have lots of friends, but no one to really talk to. There's no one in my class I can talk to. Then I go home at night and the house feels empty. Grandma sits there silent as the grave. Daddy's always working in London – I hardly ever see him. Mummy's thousands of miles away.'

'You don't have to be top of things to feel lonely,' said Marina. 'Lots of people feel that.'

'No, but it makes you *different*: people expect so much of you,' said Verena.

'That's partly because you expect so much of yourself,' countered Marina.

Verena smiled. 'True.'

'And people wouldn't expect things of you, if they didn't think you could do them.'

'Also true – but it still doesn't stop you feeling lonely,' said Verena. 'I'm so glad I can talk to you about things.'

'Me, too,' said Marina. They talked for another minute, then it was time for lessons.

'Okay, catch you later,' said Verena and off they went.

A few seconds later, as Verena rounded the corner of the Quad, she passed Flame Sprite. The two girls gave each other a wary glance and seemed to move further apart as they crossed.

Just after the Sprite Sisters left for school that morning, the engineers arrived at Sprite Towers and parked their lorry on the lawn beside the fountain. Then they began to set their equipment to drill down into the earth. Attached to the back of the lorry was a huge metal frame that opened up and now stood, like a tripod, about twenty feet high. In the middle of the frame was an auger – a huge drill shaped like a corkscrew – which would be powered by a motor in the back of the lorry.

Dad came out to talk to the men. He was pleased to learn that the head engineer thought Sprite Towers could probably have its own supply of pure, fresh drinking water.

The head engineer took some samples for testing, then gave instructions to the foreman and left.

By late morning, everything was ready for the drilling to begin. The motor started and the auger whirred – they made a lot of noise, but it was exciting. Dad watched, absorbed, his hands in the pockets of his big old garden jacket, as the auger drilled into the soil.

Then, suddenly, there was a terrible screeching sound. Dad put his hands up over his ears.

Charlie, the foreman, lifted his arm in the air and peered into the hole. 'Whoa – 'old up thar!' he shouted, in his broad Norfolk accent.

The workmen turned off the engine.

'What's the matter?' asked Dad, moving forwards.

'We've hit something!' shouted Charlie. 'Bring it up!'

The auger was raised, leaving a narrow hole in the grass.

In the sudden silence, Dad wondered what they would do now.

Then he drew a sharp breath. Something dark seemed to

rise up out of the hole in the ground.

Dad stared. First he thought it was smoke or some sort of gas being released. Then he thought it looked like a shadow. Whatever it was seemed to spin round slowly in a whirl, a black, whirling shadow. Dad shuddered. It didn't feel nice.

Dad looked up, saw Charlie's eyes widen. He's seen it, too, he thought, and noticed the way the man's gaze followed the shadow as it came out of the hole and seemed to whirl around Charlie's feet.

A cold shiver ran right through Dad's body. He was transfixed, unable to move, aware that the shadow was now moving towards him. Over the grass it came, twisting and thrashing, like a black angry ball.

Dad felt his fingers go cold as ice as the shadow moved towards him over the ground. As it got closer, it rose up, seeming to swirl around his shoulders and face.

A deep pit seemed to form in his stomach, making him feel a little giddy. Dad saw the workmen watch him – registered the look of horror on their faces – as the dark, spinning ball moved around his face.

Then, just as he felt his heart would stop, the dark shadow moved away over the grass.

It's going towards the house, thought Dad. Still he was unable to move. Another cold shiver ran right through his body.

He stared as the shadow approached the back door.

'No!' shouted Dad – and he began to run towards it. 'No, don't let it in!'

But it was too late. Grandma had opened the kitchen door,

and was standing there calling him for lunch. Dad stared in horror as the dark shadow swirled around her – then streamed past her, through the door into Sprite Towers.

Oh my God, thought Dad. Whatever have we done?

'What was that?' shouted Charlie.

'God knows!' said Dad, and he ran towards the house.

Grandma had been preparing the lunch in the kitchen. Archie was licking Bert, who was lying in his basket by the Aga. Pudding the cat lay curled up on the Windsor chair, uninterested in the dogs. Grandma had laid out the cheese on a plate, dressed the salad and put out one of Mum's homemade loaves of bread. She had called Mum, who was coming down the stairs. Dad was still out there in the garden, watching the engineers. Right, she thought, I'll just call him in, then we can eat – and she moved towards the kitchen door.

As Grandma's hand turned the handle, she had the sudden sensation that she should not have opened the door – but it was too late. As the cool autumn air hit her face, something else – something dark like a shadow, something icy cold that made the pit of her stomach drop, something that seemed to stick to the skin on her face – moved past her. Grandma stood transfixed, staring at the 'thing', as it swirled across the kitchen towards the hall door. In his basket, little Archie whined, as if in pain. Bert yelped. The hair on their backs stood up straight.

And then, Ottalie Sprite opened the door from the hallway and breezed into the kitchen. Grandma saw the smile on her daughter-in-law's face change into a look of fear, as the dark energy swirled past her.

'What was *that*?' said Mum, in a shuddering voice.

'I don't know, dear,' said Grandma, moving towards her. 'But whatever it is, it's gone into the house.'

The two women stared into the hall. 'I feel all cold and shaky,' said Mum.

'So do I,' said Grandma.

They turned as Dad walked into the kitchen through the open door, and saw their white faces.

'Did you see it?' he asked.

'What was it?' asked Mum, noticing that his face was pale, too. 'It was as if something really horrible moved past me and into the house.'

'Did it look like a dark shadow?' asked Dad.

'I didn't really see it – it was all so quick. But it felt like that, yes,' replied Mum.

'Did you see it, Ma?' he asked his mother.

'Yes – and I felt it, too,' she said, giving a slight shudder. 'The dogs saw it as well. They didn't like it a bit – their hair stood on end.'

They stood there, silent, for a moment.

Then Dad said, 'What shall we do?'

Grandma looked at him. 'I don't think there is anything we can do, dear – except hope it's gone away.'

Then Mum, ever practical, said, 'Well, let's have some lunch.'

They were all quite quiet at the table. Then Mum said, 'I don't think we should say anything to the girls.'

Dad nodded. 'Okay, if you say so.'

Grandma was silent. She knew her granddaughters would feel the dark power that had passed into the house. They will feel it as soon as they walk in, she thought. Their magic powers will make them aware. You can't hide it from them.

But what is it? she wondered. And why is it here?

As Mum drove the girls back from school later that afternoon, Flame noticed her mother was subdued. They asked her about the engineers – and she told them they'd started to drill a hole in the lawn. Then they were all quiet.

Ash half listened, but stared out of the car window, deep in thought. Marina seemed absorbed too, thought Flame. Ariel was in her usual dream.

Flame was first out of the car and opened the front door. As soon as she stepped through, she sensed that something had changed in the house. As they walked in, her sisters felt it too.

'Weird,' said Marina, her blue eyes wide.

A querying look passed over Ariel's face, as if she couldn't quite make something out. Ash stood still and gazed up the stairs.

Mum seemed to take no notice and told them to hang up their coats and come and have some tea.

First, though, they wanted to see what was happening in the garden. The engineers had just left, but they raced over the lawn and looked at the drill.

Five minutes later, they came back, breathless and hungry.

In the kitchen, Grandma cut them slices of her homemade fruitcake, while Mum poured mugs of tea. Archie bumbled around their feet, underneath the table.

'It's all so exciting!' said Ariel.

'Yes,' said Mum. And she told them the engineers had hit something hard – perhaps the foundations of an old house that was there before Sprite Towers. She did not mention the dark, swirling shadow.

The sisters listened, but none of them said anything about the strange sensation in the house.

Ash sat silent. I must ask Grandma about the house under the garden as soon as possible, she thought.

After tea, Marina wanted to talk to Mum about Verena. Ariel wanted to play with Archie, who was only allowed in the kitchen until he learned to stop piddling everywhere. Flame and Ash climbed the stairs and walked from room to room.

'There's a strange feeling in this house,' said Ash, opening a bedroom door.

'Yes,' agreed Flame. But neither of them saw anything as they walked around. Neither of them sensed a dark shadow. Whatever it was that had entered was now well hidden in the big house.

Meanwhile, in the kitchen, Marina sat and talked to her mother. She explained what Verena had said to her earlier that day. Mum listened and was, as Marina predicted, concerned. 'Tell her to come and talk to me,' she said.

'I already have, Mum.'

'Good.'

That evening, after Mum said goodnight, Marina, Ash and Ariel crept through to Flame's room and sat on her bed.

Marina told her sisters what Verena had told her. She watched Flame – noticed her sister's face soften a little – but knew it was still too early for Flame to be friends with her rival. Verena had caused a deep rift between her and Flame that summer. It was healed now, but the memory was still there. I must give her more time, thought Marina.

Then they talked about the feeling in the house. What was it? Was it connected to the water and the men drilling in the ground?

Ash thought so. 'I've a feeling something was released when the engineers made the hole in the ground. I felt last night that something was going to happen.'

Ariel lifted her chin. 'Do you think . . .' she said. 'Do you think that things happen to us because we have magic powers? Or do you think that because we have magic powers, we make things happen?'

Flame, Marina and Ash smiled. 'Ariel, you are endlessly surprising,' said Flame. 'That's a deep question.'

'Well, I think it's interesting,' said Ariel. 'You see, I wonder why all these things keep happening to us. I mean, are all the children in my class feeling something weird in their houses this evening? Do they all get attacked every now and then by people with dark power like Glenda Glass? Or do they go home and watch the telly?'

Just then the bedroom door opened. Thankfully, it was not Mum, who would have got cross. It was Grandma.

'What is it that's in the house?' asked Flame, as she sat down on the bed.

'I don't know,' replied Grandma, her face thoughtful.

'How did it get in?' asked Marina.

'Your father saw something coming out of the hole the men were drilling,' said Grandma. 'He was quite shaken up by it. The men were, too. Your father said it was like a swirling black shadow and he saw it move towards the house. I happened to open the back door, to call him in for lunch. I certainly felt it move past me. Your mother felt it, too, when she opened the hall door to come into the kitchen.'

'Mum felt it?' said Flame, with a look of surprise. 'Mum never feels things like that!'

Grandma's face was thoughtful. 'Well, she did today, love.'

'So you *all* saw or felt it,' said Ash, her brown eyes serious.

'What did it feel like?' asked Flame.

Grandma grimaced. 'It wasn't nice.'

'Is it something to do with Glenda Glass?' asked Marina.

'I don't know,' replied Grandma. 'I think it's more likely to be some sort of energy that's been trapped in the ground. Glenda may be able to feel it, too. We must wait and see.'

'It's made you nervous,' said Ariel.

Grandma smiled a small smile. 'Come on, it's time for bed.'

'But Grandma, I wanted to ask you about the house under the garden before you leave for France,' said Ash.

'I know you do, love, but it'll have to wait – your mother said she'd be up again to check you're all settling down.'

Grandma kissed Flame goodnight. As her sisters walked back to their rooms, Mum appeared at the top of the stairs.

Grandma followed Ash to her room. As she climbed into bed, Ash whispered, 'I've a feeling that the old house under the garden is connected to the thing that's in the house now.'

Grandma nodded. 'I think you're right. We'll talk about it soon. Come on, school in the morning.'

'Night, Grandma.'

'Night, love.'

Ash snuggled down under her duvet, but her mind was racing. As she lay in the dark, she thought about the men drilling through the ground and her father seeing the strange energy whirl up and move over the garden. She imagined it moving through the house.

It could be in this room, here, now, she thought – and she sat up, quickly, turned on the light and looked around.

For a minute, she watched, waited. It's not in here, she thought. I'm safe.

Then she reached out to switch off the light and snuggled down once more.

CHAPTER FOUR

GLENDA REVEALS

ON WEDNESDAY evening at The Oaks, Glenda Glass felt restless. What is it, she wondered as she walked about the house with her long, dancer's strides. Something is happening. Something is . . . something is *moving*, she thought. And it's something connected to *me* . . .

The image of Sprite Towers flashed into her mind. The Sprites, she thought. It's something to do with the Sprites . . .

She gazed out of the window at the garden, smoothed the chignon of pale blond hair at the nape of her neck with her long fingers. Again the restlessness returned, and she moved to smooth the cushions on the sofa.

There was something else on Glenda's mind. She felt certain that Verena had received an important email from her mother,

Zoe, in South America. She had not seen it, just sensed its existence. That her granddaughter had been even more distant than usual the last few days heightened her suspicion that something was afoot. I will ask her this evening, she thought.

Later, as they ate supper, Glenda suddenly asked, 'How is your mother?'

Verena started, surprised. She was about to reply when Glenda stated, 'You've heard from her.' She left the words hanging in the air.

Verena waited a few seconds, then said, 'Yes, I have.'

'I thought so. And?'

Glenda's eyes were watchful. Verena took a deep breath. 'Mummy . . . Mummy wants to come home.'

'Really. How interesting.'

'I think it's wonderful, not "interesting",' said Verena, with as much ice in her tone as she could muster.

Glenda smiled a cold smile. 'I expect your mother is tired of her Argentinian boyfriend.'

Verena gasped. 'You've never liked my mother,' she said, quietly.

Glenda glanced at her granddaughter. 'She left my son in the lurch. What do you expect me to feel?'

Verena had no answer to this. It was true: her mother had upped and left her father, suddenly. She had never understood why, as they seemed to love each other. Her father was still sad and baffled as to what had happened.

But Glenda knew. She knew exactly – because she had caused the rift.

She had been living in the south of France, but wanted to come home to be close to her son, Stephen. Through his life, she had hardly taken any notice of him. But now she was older, Glenda found she wanted his love.

Besides, she wanted to come back to be close to Sprite Towers. There was magic power to be found in the huge old house, and she aimed to have it.

But Zoe was a problem. Daughter-in-law and mother-in-law had never got on.

Better that Zoe was out of the way, Glenda had decided. And so, deliberately, she soured her son's marriage. Using her dark magic power, Glenda filled Zoe and Stephen with negative, angry thoughts.

Almost overnight, they were changed people – and their marriage suffered terribly. They began to argue all the time, although neither knew why. Stephen grew angry and moody. Zoe was hurt and suspicious. She believed her husband no longer loved her. He believed she no longer loved him.

Within a few months, Glenda drove away Zoe, who fled to South America and an old boyfriend. To the world it appeared as if her daughter-in-law was to blame for the failed marriage.

Neither Stephen, nor Zoe, had any idea that Glenda had poisoned their love.

Glenda had broken the Sprite Code of Honour – the old, unspoken law in the family that magic power was only to be used for good. But Glenda did not care. She had only ever been interested in getting what she wanted. If it meant using dark power, then she used it.

And it had worked. As she had anticipated, Stephen asked her to come to The Oaks to look after Verena. He needed his mother's help, as he worked long hours in London and could only come home at weekends.

And, now, here she was sitting with her granddaughter, eating supper.

They had been sitting here eating supper like this – in virtual silence – since the early summer.

Glenda glanced at Verena. She just couldn't seem to connect with her. Her thoughts turned, instead, to Sprite Towers. Oh, how she wanted that house! How she wanted to harness the Sprite Sisters' magic power!

Every time I try to get close – every time – those girls push me back, she thought. She jabbed a small piece of chicken with her fork, then said, 'So how *is* your mother?'

Verena did not look up. 'I don't want to talk about Mummy.'

Glenda looked steadily at Verena, and saw the girl was determined. So she took another tack. 'How are the Sprites?'

Verena seemed to relax at this question, though her eyes remained on her plate of food. 'There are engineers at Sprite Towers – they're drilling a well on the lawn.'

'Oh?' said Glenda, leaning forward.

'Apparently, lots of water suddenly appeared on the Sprites' lawn. It came from under the ground and sprayed up like a fountain, so Mr Sprite called in the engineers. When they drilled down into the lawn, they hit something hard. It turned out it was the foundations of a house that had been there before Sprite Towers.'

Glenda's face turned pale.

Verena looked up. 'What's the matter, Grandma?'

Glenda stared ahead. Memories began to whirr in her mind. Sad memories. Angry memories. Memories of another time.

She placed her knife and fork on the plate with precision, dabbed her napkin on her lips. Then she turned to Verena and said, 'Did I ever tell you that our family owned the house and land at Sprite Towers before Sidney Sprite built his house?'

Verena frowned. 'No, I've never heard that.'

'Well, we did. My grandmother, Margaret, was Sidney's elder sister. They grew up in the town with their parents, Lily and Arthur. When she grew up, Margaret married a man named Thomas Hunt, and they bought the house that was in the garden of what became Sprite Towers. They had two daughters, my mother, Harriet, and my aunt, Agatha, who were both born at the house.'

Verena listened, intrigued. 'What was the house like?'

'It was very old – Tudor, I believe,' replied Glenda. 'It was built of brick and had very high brick chimneys. I saw an old photograph of it once.'

'Did you ever go there?'

'No. This happened before I was born. My mother told me about it, many years later.'

'So what happened to this house?'

'Well,' said Glenda, conscious she had her granddaughter's attention. 'Thomas's business failed and he lost all his money. By that time, Sidney had become a rich man through his toffee manufacturing business. He had married Mim and had several children and wanted to build a house. He wanted to build a big house – something really grand. So he offered to buy Thomas and Margaret's house and the land around it. They accepted, of course – they had no choice, as they needed the money. They bought a small house in town and opened up a fruit shop.'

'And Sidney Sprite built Sprite Towers?'

'Yes. He razed the old house to the ground – they were good at knocking down old things to make way for new houses in those days – and he built this massive house with its high towers. I believe it was finished in 1910.'

'Did Margaret mind?'

Glenda looked at Verena with a steady gaze. 'Yes, she minded a lot. She missed her home. She and Sidney had always got on when they were children, but as they grew up they grew apart.'

Verena looked thoughtful. Glenda pondered whether to tell her granddaughter that Sidney had paid Thomas and Margaret handsomely for their house – which had been in a terrible state of repair – but decided not to. Better that Verena think that Sidney's side of the family were a mean lot, she thought.

'Then Thomas died,' continued Glenda. 'Margaret was left with very little money and two children to support. She worked very hard. She wanted to go and live at Sprite Towers with her brother, but Sidney refused to let her come there ever again.'

'But that's awful!' said Verena. 'Her *own* brother!'

Glenda nodded.

'But why?'

'I don't know – but it was a terrible way to treat his sister and her daughters.'

'So where did they go?'

'Margaret rented a small place in the town and struggled to raise her children,' replied Glenda. 'I was a little girl when she died, but I do remember her. She was a very strong woman, but they say she died of a broken heart. She'd lost her house, her husband – and then her brother's love.'

'I wonder if the Sprite Sisters know this story,' said Verena.

'I doubt it,' said Glenda, drily. 'I imagine they've only heard the nice things about Sidney Sprite.'

'He was famous for being a kind man, our history teacher said,' said Verena. 'She said he looked after his factory workers well, built lots of houses for them and gave them hot lunches and medical care. And Miss Sapwell said he gave a lot of money to the local school and hospital.'

'Well, dear, there's always two sides to a story,' said Glenda.

Verena was silent for a moment. Then she said, 'Did Sidney really stop Margaret coming to the house?'

'Yes,' replied Glenda. 'And she never forgave him.'

'It's a sad story,' said Verena.

'Well, often people who make a lot of money are ruthless and mean,' said Glenda.

Verena flushed. 'Daddy's made a lot of money – and he's not mean or ruthless! And *you* have a lot of money. Are *you* ruthless and mean?'

Glenda's cold blue eyes met Verena's. The girl gasped at the power in that gaze – and looked down.

'There's no need to be rude, Verena.'

'I'm not being rude,' Verena retorted. 'I'm asking an honest question.'

'I take your point, dear,' said Glenda, picking up the plates and getting up from the table. 'Now, shall we get on? I expect you've got some homework.'

Verena got up and cleared the glasses and mats from the table. As she turned towards the kitchen, her grandmother was waiting. 'Verena – I'd like you to keep me up to date on what's happening at Sprite Towers.'

Verena looked at her grandmother, met the cold, hard gaze once again. It was not the first time that Glenda had asked for information about the Sprites.

'Find out as much as you can – and tell me what's going on up there,' said Glenda, then she turned and went into the kitchen.

Verena stood for a few seconds. I miss Mummy, she thought. I really miss her . . .

That night, as Verena lay in bed, she thought about Margaret's story. She did not trust her grandmother, but this story sounded real. So *her* family had owned Sprite Towers! How extraordinary, she thought.

It explains why Grandma dislikes the Sprites so much, she thought. But how could Sidney have treated her great-great-grandmother so badly? That was not how her teacher described him – and the Sprite family she knew all seemed such nice people. She was fond of Mr and Mrs Sprite and of Marina. Even Flame, who she did not much like, was regarded as a good person by everyone at school. But the Sprite Sisters were related to a man who had been cruel to her great-great-grandmother. Sidney had banished Margaret from his house. That was an awful thing to do.

Verena gazed into the dark. Strange to think I might have been sleeping now in the house at Sprite Towers, not here at The Oaks . . .

Her thoughts turned to her mother. I will cycle over and talk to Mrs Sprite at the weekend. I must talk to a grown-up who I trust, who knows Mummy and understands these things. I so want Mummy to come home . . .

As Verena fell asleep, Glenda sat in the drawing room on the cream silk sofa.

I need information, she thought. She picked up the phone and dialled a number.

In London, Charles Smythson answered his phone.

'Charles – it's Glenda,' she announced. 'I want you to do something for me.'

Without stopping to ask Charles if he would help her, Glenda explained that a spring had appeared at Sprite Towers and that the foundations of the old house had come to light. She demanded that he visit as soon as possible, to find out what was happening.

Glenda Glass's nephew sank into the nearest chair and listened as his aunt ranted on about the Sprite family.

As an art historian, Charles had recently completed an

inventory of the pictures of Sprite Towers and would need soon to return. As Glenda's spy, he had tried to get hold of the secret plan that unlocked some of the magic of Sprite Towers. He had failed in this, but he had given her a lot of useful information about the family. She now knew about the portal the Sprite Sisters created – the doorway to times past and future, that opened in the West Tower.

Like Glenda, Charles Smythson came from the branch of the Sprite family that had not upheld the Sprite Code of Honour. Glenda had found her nephew's weak spot: a love of and need for money. If Charles agreed to work for her, she would fund his lavish lifestyle.

Charles complied. He used his dark powers against the Sprite Sisters, learned about their magic and caused them harm. For this, Glenda Glass paid him handsomely.

But Charles had become fond of the Sprites – and anyway, he had got caught out. The girls and their grandmother had trapped him. They knew all about Charles Smythson's dark power – and who was paying him.

Marilyn Sprite had asked him many questions and forced him to think hard about the course of his life, and what was right.

Charles decided he'd had enough of Glenda Glass. With his fee from Colin Sprite, more work from Stephen Glass and his considerable fee from Glenda, he had cleared his debts and changed his lifestyle.

Recently – through Stephen Glass – he'd had a new commission. He was not about to squander his growing reputation as an art historian, to help a vengeful woman wreak yet more harm on the Sprite family.

'Enough,' Charles broke in. 'No more, Glenda.'

Glenda laughed. She was not one to give up. First she threatened, then she raised the offer of money to such high stakes that, for a moment, Charles hesitated.

He gazed over at his desk, looked at the Sprite Towers inventory sitting on the top. 'As it happens, I am going up to Sprite Towers next weekend,' he said. 'I have to give the inventory to Colin and Ottalie.'

'You must go now – you must go this weekend!'

Charles stared at the inventory on the desk. 'No – I'm tied up this coming weekend. I will go next weekend.'

'I expect results this time,' said Glenda. 'Find out what you can, then come and see me.'

Charles was silent. I loathe this woman, he thought. I loathe the power she has, the way she manipulates people.

Then, as if sensing his hesitation, Glenda said, 'You see, Charles, there have been interesting developments. New forces are at work.'

'New forces?' Charles sat forward in his chair and leaned his forehead in his hand.

Glenda laughed. 'New forces that will hurt the Sprites – and help me to get Sprite Towers.'

Charles drew breath, his jaw tightened. 'What forces?'

Glenda laughed quietly again. Then she said in a voice so low it was almost a whisper, 'Dark forces under the earth, Charles. I believe something may have been disturbed. Something which had much better been left still.'

Charles froze. Oh my God, he thought. What is she planning

now? This is the woman who has stolen Marilyn Sprite's inheritance. This is the woman who stops at nothing . . .

He knew that there were many things that upset Glenda Glass: her lifelong battle with her cousin, Marilyn, who was chosen as the prima ballerina in the ballet corps, for instance, and Marilyn's marriage to Sheldon Sprite. But the things that upset her most were not being given the 'secret' and not owning Sprite Towers.

'I want the house, Charles,' she said. 'I want the power that is in Sprite Towers. Most of all, I want the "secret" – the thing that Lily Sprite gave to Sidney. I want to know what it is and how it works. Lily should never have given it to Sidney. My grandmother was the older sister and it's *our* branch of the family that should own that power. If we don't find it now, the Sprite Sisters will.'

Charles Smythson listened. She's crazy, he thought. His head slumped into his hand. What do I do, he thought. What do I do? He remembered how the Sprite Sisters had found the magic box, which contained the secret plan that allowed the girls to create the portal. He had failed to bring Glenda the plan. The Sprite Sisters still had this.

Then he drew breath. 'Glenda – what is this "secret" you're talking about? I thought the portal was the secret. Now you're saying there's more?'

'Yes, Charles, there's more.'

'So what *is* it?'

'Lily showed Sidney a way to enhance the Sprites' magic power many, many times. My mother told me it was a way to make the power go right through the family. It's connected to the plan the girls have. I believe it reveals more than the portal – and that's why I want it. We have to find it!'

Charles sighed. This is going to go on and on, he thought, gloomily. Just as I get my life sorted out, Glenda's banging on again. Why doesn't she just give up . . .

At The Oaks, Glenda looked across the elegant drawing room. She focused her mind on Margaret Sprite. She remembered stories of her grandmother's power. It was said to be terrifying. I can feel the power moving, she thought. It is moving through Sprite Towers . . .

In London, Charles heard the line click and the tone turn to a hum. For some while, he sat there, holding his phone, staring into space.

Glenda cradled the phone in her hand, a satisfied smile on her face.

CHAPTER FIVE

THE
SHADOW

AT SPRITE Towers on Thursday evening, Mum and Dad were getting ready to go out to supper with some friends. Mum was in the shower, Dad was putting on his smart trousers and shirt.

He tucked in the shirt, then pulled at a loose cuff, muttered, 'Cufflinks,' and walked across the bedroom to a tall chest of drawers. He peered down at a small leather tray on the top of the chest, where he kept his cufflinks and watch.

'Have you seen my gold cufflinks?' he asked, as Mum walked through.

'I expect they're in your tray,' she replied, rubbing her wavy blond hair with a towel.

'No, they're not there.' Dad scratched his head.

'Jacket?' suggested Mum.

'Why would I have put them there?'

Mum shrugged. 'Maybe you took them off somewhere out of the house, and put them in a pocket for safekeeping.'

Dad screwed up his face, as if to say, 'Don't be daft!'

For the next ten minutes, he hunted everywhere. He opened all the drawers, went through every little box, but the cufflinks were nowhere to be found.

'When did you last see them?' asked Mum.

Dad rubbed his chin. 'I could have sworn I saw them in the tray this morning.'

'Let's go through all your pockets,' she suggested.

A few minutes later, Dad went downstairs to the kitchen. Grandma and the Sprite Sisters were sitting at the table, eating their supper. Archie was trying to lick Bert, who was having none of it.

'Has anyone seen my gold cufflinks?' asked Dad.

Everyone shook their head. 'Sorry, Dad,' said Flame.

'Perhaps they're in the car?' suggested Marina.

'Jacket pocket?' suggested Grandma.

'No, Ottalie and I have just gone through those,' said Dad. 'They seem to have vanished into thin air.' And he walked out, back up to the bedroom to find a substitute pair of cufflinks for his shirt.

Grandma looked thoughtful.

'What's the matter, Grandma?' asked Flame.

'I was just thinking that I couldn't find my pen this afternoon. I keep it on my desk, as you know. I looked for it everywhere.'

'Did you find it?' asked Marina.

Grandma shook her head. 'No, but I'm sure it will turn up.'

Ash leaned forward, her brown eyes wide. 'So Grandma, tell us about the house under the garden. I thought we'd never get you on your own!'

Grandma smiled. The Sprite Sisters waited, attentive. Then she started to tell them about the old, old house under the garden. The story she told began just as the story that Glenda Glass had told Verena the evening before – but then it changed.

'Margaret Sprite's husband, Thomas, was a lazy drunk,' said Grandma. 'Nobody knew why she married him. He spent all their money and drank it away – so that they had to sell their house.'

Sidney Sprite had indeed bought the old house and the land, explained Grandma. But where Glenda had inferred to Verena that Sidney had been mean, Grandma was quick to point out that he gave Thomas and Margaret a large sum of money for their house.

'Sidney gave them a lot more for the house than it was worth,' said Grandma. 'He was a good man, and he wanted to make sure his sister and her children would be provided for.'

Thomas and Margaret moved into town and opened their fruit shop, she explained, but he kept drinking and that business failed, too. Then Thomas died and things got even worse. It was difficult for Sidney, Grandma explained. He and Margaret had been close when they were children and as young adults. Then, when they grew up, they both developed the magic power that runs through the Sprite family.

The Sprite Sisters listened, all ears.

'Sidney's power was very strong,' said Grandma.

'Margaret's power was equally strong. They both knew and understood that their magic must only be used for good: their mother, Lily, had always been very strict on this. But Margaret made a bad choice in her husband and her life began to get difficult. She began to explore dark magic – perhaps she thought this would help her situation. Sidney did not like Thomas and he was unhappy that his sister had made a poor choice in her marriage. He was very worried when he heard Margaret had turned towards dark power. When he bought their house and gave them money, Sidney hoped that Thomas and Margaret would have a better life.

'But Thomas began to drink more and more – and died,' said Grandma. 'Margaret's moods became darker and darker and she used her powers against people. She became bitter and jealous, angry that her life had gone sour.'

'So what happened?' asked Ariel.

'Well, there was another factor in all this, apart from the money,' said Grandma. 'And that was who would hold the secret of the Sprite magic power.'

'Isn't that the plan we found this summer?' asked Flame.

'I believe the plan is part of it. But there was something else.'

'Another portal?' asked Ariel with wide eyes.

Grandma shook her head. 'I don't know for sure, love, but I think it was a way to increase the power in the family.'

'Is there another plan?' asked Marina.

'Or is it something to do with my magic stone?' asked Ash. She drew the stone out of her pocket and held it on the palm of her hand. They all looked at it.

'Possibly,' nodded Grandma. 'I don't know.'

'So how will we find it?' asked Marina.

'Or how will we stop Glenda finding it?' interrupted Flame. 'Where there's a secret or a plan Glenda is never far behind.' She stared down, biting her lip.

They were all silent for a moment, then Ariel piped up, 'Grandma, tell us about this Margaret person. What's she got to do with us?'

Marilyn Sprite smiled at her granddaughter. 'Now where was I . . . ah yes. I wasn't there, of course – this was some time before I was born – but this was what my mother told me. She said that Lily Sprite, Sidney and Margaret's mother, held some kind of special knowledge about the Sprite power – something that had been in the family for many generations, long before Sprite Towers was built.'

'So it's some kind of ancient magic?' asked Flame.

'I believe so.'

'How far back does the Sprite magic go?' asked Ash.

'A long, long way.'

'So what happened to this "secret" thing?' asked Ariel.

'Well, Lily knew that some day she would have to hand this on to one of her children, as was the Sprite tradition,' said Grandma. 'As the eldest child, Margaret assumed her mother would give it to her. Just before Sidney built Sprite Towers in 1910, Lily became ill and knew she might die – so she had to make the choice. I'm not sure if any of Lily and Arthur's other children had the power, but as far as I know Lily felt it was a choice between Margaret and Sidney. Lily knew that Margaret had moved towards dark power – and she dare not risk giving the secret to her.'

'So she gave it to Sidney,' said Flame.

Grandma nodded. 'Yes – Lily gave the secret to Sidney.'

'Was Margaret very angry?' asked Ash.

'She was furious.'

'Was this before she lost her house?' asked Flame.

'I believe so, but when she lost the house she got even angrier.'

'She must have been really horrible,' said Ariel.

'She wasn't happy.'

'I'm not surprised she was angry,' said Flame. 'She didn't get the secret – and she was married to a man who lost their house and money, then lost the second lot of money that Sidney had given them.'

'It's a sad story,' agreed Grandma. 'But it was Margaret's choice. Sidney tried to help her. It was she who chose dark power. As I always tell you, our magic is a wonderful gift. The Sprites who have the "good" magic power must always use it wisely. As you know, I had power and I lost it in the fight with Glenda Glass forty-five years ago.'

'But you were only trying to defend yourself, Grandma,' countered Flame.

'I don't understand why you lost your magic power, Grandma, but Glenda didn't,' said Ariel.

'Nor did this Margaret person, from what you say,' added Ash.

A sad look passed over Grandma's face. 'It's just one of those things, girls. Maybe good magic power is more fragile, as it is so precious.'

'Did you ever meet Margaret?' asked Marina.

'I knew her when I was a little girl. She was an old lady by then.'

'What was she like?'

'She had long black hair and very dark eyes – she was a handsome woman. But, as she got older and less happy, she had a temper and could suddenly be sharp with people. You never knew which way she would turn.'

'Were you frightened of her?' asked Ash.

'I never felt comfortable around her.'

'Did you know she had magic power?' asked Flame.

'Not until I was older and had it myself,' replied Grandma. 'The Sprites are very quiet about their power, if they have it. Not all of them have, of course – like your father and grandfather. Neither of them has had magic power.'

'So what happened to Margaret?' asked Ash.

Grandma turned to her. 'Well, things got worse and worse. Sidney had built Sprite Towers. He had this lovely new house, lots of children and was a well-known man in the town. He wanted to help his sister, but he refused to whilst she worked with dark power. He asked her to work only with good power, to help people.'

'Did they argue?' asked Ariel.

'Yes,' replied Grandma. 'They argued more and more. Sidney begged her, but Margaret refused to give up dark magic. She had become so bitter that she blamed Sidney for her misfortunes. My mother told me Margaret got so jealous that she tried to hurt Sidney.'

'How?' asked Marina.

'She caused an accident that broke his leg – and several

times he fell seriously ill, without any apparent reason. He was a strong man.'

The Sprite Sisters looked shocked. 'That's awful!' said Ash.

Grandma nodded. 'In the end, Sidney was so upset that he told Margaret never to come to Sprite Towers again.'

'She was banished?' asked Flame.

'Something like that,' said Grandma.

They were all silent. 'That's dreadful,' said Flame, staring down at the floor.

Then Ariel looked at Grandma and suddenly piped up. 'So what's this strange dark thing that Dad and you saw come into the house?'

Grandma gazed at Ariel for a moment, then she said quietly, 'I don't know.'

'Has anyone seen it again?' asked Ariel.

'Not as far as I know,' replied Grandma. 'Neither of your parents have said anything about it today. Hopefully, it's gone away.'

'Dad said he thought that what the engineers came across under the lawn were the remains of the cellar of the old house,' said Flame.

'Yes, that makes sense,' said Grandma. 'Cellars are built underground, so they're often left when a house is pulled down.'

'Do you think Margaret fell through a hole in the lawn and fell into the old cellar and got trapped there – and *died*?' asked Ariel, her eyes wide as saucers. 'Or maybe Sidney murdered her with an axe and left her body to rot!'

They all burst out laughing. 'Ariel!' exclaimed Marina.

The girls glanced at their grandmother. Marilyn Sprite's face had the smallest hint of a smile. 'As far as I know, Margaret Sprite died in the town,' she said. 'I've *never* heard any story about anybody being murdered or dying in a cellar at Sprite Towers.'

'Well, that's a relief!' said Flame.

'I think it's a good story,' retorted Ariel, her ski-jump nose in the air.

'Doesn't make it true!' said Marina.

Just then Dad walked in through the door, wearing his jacket and tie. 'Cor, you look smart, Dad!' said Marina.

'Did you find the cufflinks?' asked Grandma.

'Unfortunately, no,' said Dad, sitting down at the table and stroking Archie, who had bumbled over and crawled on to his foot.

'What did the engineers say about the water?' asked Flame.

Colin Sprite smiled at his eldest daughter. 'Good news – the tests show the water is pure.'

'So we can drink it?' said Marina.

'Yes, it will be piped into the house,' said Dad.

'Fantastic!' said Flame.

'There's ever so much water out there on the lawn still, Dad,' said Ash. 'It looks like we've had a flood.'

Dad stopped stroking Archie and looked at Ash. 'Hm, I know. The engineers are perplexed – say they've never seen a borehole produce so much water, so suddenly.'

'Will it go down?' asked Marina.

'I certainly hope so,' laughed Dad.

For a moment, Marina wondered whether to use her

magic power to help the water move, but something in her told her to wait for the engineers. They will fix it, she thought. I don't need to worry. Besides, I might risk my magic being found out – and I must keep it secret.

They all turned as Mum walked in in a short red dress and black heels. Her blond wavy hair was piled up on to her head and her bright red lipstick matched the dress. They all jumped up.

'Wow, Mum, you look *fab*!' said Marina.

'Amazing!' said Flame.

'Thank you!' beamed Mum.

'Beautiful,' said Dad, leaning down to kiss her on the cheek.

Ottalie Sprite kissed each of her daughters.

'Have fun,' said Grandma and off they went.

The Sprite Sisters helped their grandmother to clear up, then Flame and Ash went to do their music practice. Marina and Ariel had done their practice before supper and, after giving Archie a cuddle, they decided to go and find some dressing-up clothes for their Hallowe'en party the following week. As they walked up the wide mahogany staircase to the attics, Marina was thinking about Mum's red dress and hoping she could wear it some day. Ariel chattered away.

'I'm so pleased Mum's letting us have a party,' said Ariel. 'It'll be such fun to play Sardines and hide all over the house!'

'Hm,' agreed Marina, lost in the thought of being grown-up enough to dress like Mum and pile up her dark curly hair on her head. I'd wear long, dangly earrings, she thought.

Ariel was wittering on about toffee apples and pumpkins,

as they reached the third floor and turned right along the attics corridor to the dressing-up room. Marina opened the door, switched on the light and they walked in.

'I want to dress up as a skeleton,' said Ariel.

'Well, you'll need black tights and a black jumper and a black hat that covers your whole face,' said Marina. 'Then you cut out pieces of luminous white paper in the shape of bones and stick them on the black. In the dark, they'll glow.'

'So, what am I looking for now?' asked Ariel.

'A balaclava or a woolly black hat that you can roll down over your face and cut out some eyeholes.'

'And what are you looking for?'

'I'm not sure, yet. Something spooky.'

The dressing-up room was a wonderful room for a rummage and for the next ten minutes, both girls had their heads down in the various chests. Every now and then, Marina threw out a garment on the floor. They were happy and relaxed.

Nothing could have prepared the girls for what happened next.

Ariel had just found a black balaclava and turned to show Marina. But, as she did so, she screamed loudly. 'EEEEK!'

Instantly, Marina pulled herself out of the box and spun round.

Ariel's face was white and her mouth hung open like a fish. She started jabbering, pointing across the room.

Marina looked to where her sister was pointing. 'Hell's bells,' she whispered, as the colour drained from her face.

The two sisters stared across the room.

Hovering in the air was a big white hat covered with big pink flowers – the sort of thing Grandma would have worn in the 1960s.

Ariel felt her heart pounding, but she could not speak.

Marina could not move a muscle. She felt pinned to the ground as she stared at the hovering hat. In front of her face, she noticed that her breath was making clouds of mist in the air. Then she shivered. 'It's so cold!' she said, through chattering teeth.

Suddenly Ariel was shouting. '*The hat – it's moving!*'

The white and pink hat began to float towards them. As if by instinct, Marina turned her head quickly to look behind her – and noticed a dark shadow on the wall. Clearly defined on the cream plaster was the shadow of a huge, swirling shape that seemed to have no form. In front of them, however, there was nothing there to cast a shadow – only a hat hovering in the air, now just in front of their faces.

Ariel thought she would faint, her heart was beating so hard.

Marina's body felt like ice.

The hat hovered closer – and closer.

Then, just as it was about to touch Ariel's face, it moved up and down, round and round and moved – whoosh! – towards the door.

The two girls watched, transfixed, as the hat floated through the open door and out of the room.

Instantly, Marina found her feet and her voice. 'Follow it!' she shouted, running out of the door. The hat was floating at high speed along the corridor towards the small wooden door that led to the West Tower.

Then Ariel was behind her. The two girls watched as the latch lifted, as if moved by an invisible hand, and the door creaked open. The hat floated through the door.

'*Get the others!*' shouted Marina.

Ariel ran to the top of the stairs, leaned over and shrieked, '*Flame! Ash! Grandma!*'

Within seconds her sisters were pounding up the stairs.

'What's happened?' shouted Flame.

'Blimey, you're as white as a sheet!' gasped Ash.

Grandma followed close behind. 'What is it?'

Marina pointed to the door of the West Tower. 'We were in the dressing-up room,' she said, her voice going so fast she was almost in knots. 'Suddenly, there was this pink and white hat in the air! There was nothing holding it up – but it was *moving*! It came right up to our faces, but neither of us could move. The air went really cold – we could see our breath in the air. And there was this shadow. I *saw* it on the wall – only there was nothing there to make a shadow!'

'I saw the shadow, too,' whispered Ariel, clutching her grandmother tight.

'Where did the hat go?' asked Flame.

Ariel pointed to the open tower door. 'Up there,' she whispered.

Grandma drew a sharp breath. Flame moved forward to the door. 'No, Flame – I'll go first,' said her grandmother.

'I'll be right behind you.' Flame stood back, as Marilyn Sprite opened the little wooden door wide.

'And I'm right behind you,' said Ash.

One by one, they climbed the rickety wooden steps. At the top, Grandma clicked the light switch, pushed open a second small wooden door and stepped up into the tower room.

Grandma walked forward and stood, silent, in the middle of the wooden floor.

'It's empty!' cried Flame, spinning around.

'Where's the hat gone?' shouted Ash.

Marina and Ariel came through the door at the top of the rickety staircase.

'Are you sure it was this tower?' asked Flame.

Marina and Ariel nodded, speechless.

'A pink and white hat, you say?' said Grandma.

'Yes,' replied Marina, quietly.

'That was my hat,' said Grandma, looking round the room. 'It's been in the dressing-up box for years. Goodness knows where it's been spirited away to – but it's clearly not here.'

'But we saw it! We both saw it!' cried Ariel.

Grandma put her hand on Ariel's shoulder. 'I believe you, love.'

They stood quite still. Ariel and Marina looked shaky and pale. Flame put her arm around Marina.

Ash moved a few paces away and gazed around the room. In her right jeans pocket, she pulled out the magic stone that she always carried with her and laid it on her hand. Sometimes the stone emitted a squeak to alert her. At others, a bright blue light shone from it.

Ash watched the stone. 'Look,' she said, softly.

Her sisters and Grandma gathered around her, staring at the stone on her outstretched palm.

'It's changing colour,' said Ash.

Flame peered at the stone. 'How strange . . . I can see a swirling black shape.'

'So can I,' said Ash.

The others nodded. Then each looked around the room.

'There's nothing here,' said Flame.

Then Grandma broke in. 'Come on, let's go down. There's nothing we can do – and Archie will be wondering where we've all gone.'

They moved to the tower door. Grandma led the way down. Ash was last to leave.

As she was about to climb on to the top stair, the magic stone – still in her hand – emitted a piercing *beep*.

'Wait!' said Ash. Everyone stopped and looked at the magic stone, which glowed blue on Ash's hand. 'We've missed something,' she said and turned to walk back into the tower room. At the side of the east wall, she bent down and picked something up from the floor. Then she walked back to the stairs.

'What is it, love?' called Grandma, from the bottom step.

Ash looked down the steps and held out her hand. 'Your pen and Dad's cufflinks.'

Flame, Marina and Ariel looked amazed. Grandma drew a sharp breath.

In a few seconds, they were all down the stairs and standing in the attics corridor.

Ash handed the pen and cufflinks to Grandma. 'They were on the floor, by the wall.'

Grandma stared at the pen and cufflinks in her hand.

'Something is playing games with us.' Then she said, with an air of resolve, 'Come on, let's go down.'

Five minutes later, Flame, Marina, Ash and Grandma sat at the kitchen table, drinking mugs of hot cocoa. Ariel sat in the Windsor chair by the Aga, Archie on her lap.

Grandma sat still, thoughtful.

'We've got a ghost in the house,' said Ash.

Grandma was about to answer, as Ash went on, 'I knew there was something wrong – we all did, when we walked in from school on Wednesday. We felt it then.'

'It's Margaret Sprite, isn't it?' said Flame, looking at her grandmother.

Grandma was silent.

'Will she hurt us?' asked Ariel.

'I was so frightened,' said Marina. 'You should have seen it, Grandma – it was so weird!'

The four sisters all looked at their grandmother.

'So what do we do?' asked Flame.

Grandma looked around at each of them, her face serious, but calm. 'We wait and see what happens. In answer to your questions, yes, I think we have a ghost in the house, and, yes, it may be something to do with Margaret Sprite.'

'What does she want?' asked Ariel.

'She may just want us to talk to her and hear her side of the story,' suggested Ash.

'That's true,' agreed Grandma.

'She certainly wants us to know she is here,' said Flame.

Ariel looked pale. 'I shall feel so frightened in my room,

alone.' Ash put her arm around her.

'I want to sleep in Ash's bed, tonight,' said Ariel.

Grandma looked at Ash. 'Is that okay with you, love?'

'Yes, of course.'

'Thank you,' said Ariel.

The Sprite Sisters looked at their grandmother. She sat straight and tall. 'Listen, girls – whatever it is, this thing has not hurt you. In fact – it was almost as if it was playing a joke on us. But, if you ever feel frightened, remember you have magic powers. Use them to protect yourselves.'

She looked at her youngest granddaughter. 'Ariel, listen, when you do feel like sleeping in your own bedroom again, use your magic power to protect the space. In your mind, seal your windows and door and walls with your power: see them as barriers that nothing can cross. Then, know you are safe – and sleep. You *will* be safe. Do you understand?'

Ariel nodded. Then Grandma looked at Marina. 'How are you feeling now?'

Marina smiled a small smile. 'I'm okay, Grandma.'

'Good,' said Grandma. 'And you?' she asked, looking at Flame and Ash. They both nodded. 'Okay, well come on then – let's go upstairs. It's school in the morning and it's time for bed.'

CHAPTER SIX

THE FLYING LOAF

FLAME FELT unsettled on Friday morning as she went off to school. As Mum drove the big red car along the winding lanes, she stared out at the trees and the fields. I don't like it, she thought. Something's not right.

The experience in the tower room had given them all a shock, and Marina and Ariel were still a little shaky.

How could a solid object just *disappear*? Why had the ghost returned Dad's cufflinks and Grandma's pen and not the hat? And what would it take next?

Flame stared out at a flock of gulls following a tractor as it ploughed a field. She watched the white birds dive and swoop to pick up the worms and grubs unearthed in the newly turned furrows. Something about the way they fought and grabbed reminded her of Charles Smythson, that summer, as he'd tried to get his hands on the magic box that contained the plan of Sprite Towers.

But we outsmarted him, she thought. We kept the magic safe. Glenda did not get her hands on it.

She thought, for a moment, about the magic they had found in the house. First, they had opened a cavity hidden in the wall and discovered the magic stone. Then they had found a letter tucked behind a portrait. The stone and the letter had led the girls to the magic box, which contained the plan of Sprite Towers. And the plan led them to the portal – the door that opened in the West Tower.

Flame did not believe in coincidence. She believed that everything was connected, that nothing was random. The stone, the letter, the plan and the portal – they were all leading the Sprite Sisters somewhere.

What's next? she wondered. There is something else. Perhaps it is connected to this 'secret' that Lily passed on to Sidney?

As she gazed out of the car window, Flame thought about what she knew so far about the Sprites' magic. Grandma had told them that, many, many years ago, Lily told her son Sidney some sort of 'secret'. In doing this, thought Flame, her great-great-grandmother began a train of events that led to this moment. And that train must lead to the ghost now moving along the corridors of Sprite Towers.

Flame tried to picture how things were between Sidney and Margaret. He must have been relieved to be given the secret of the Sprite magic, she thought, but feared that his sister, Margaret, would try to get it. Sidney wanted to hand the secret on to his family – she felt sure of that, somehow. But which of them would he have given it to?

Flame thought back to how they had first found the magic stone and saved Sprite Towers from Glenda's attack. Then, as they'd been re-hanging a portrait of Mim, Sidney's wife, Ash found a letter tucked into the back of the frame.

The letter had been written – and hidden there – by George, Sidney's son, around ninety years ago in 1917. It was addressed to the four Sprite Sisters. Within weeks of writing to his descendants, George was killed in France, in the First World War.

Flame's mind began to whirr. I'll bet Sidney passed the secret to George, she thought. But he died young – so maybe he didn't have the chance to hand it on. Or did he? she wondered. Perhaps the secret is at Sprite Towers, somewhere? Sidney and George must have known we Sprite Sisters would one day live here. They must have known we would find the plan and open the portal – and they must have known we would use our power wisely.

And, thought Flame – for she liked to reason things through – it must mean they both knew that Margaret and her relatives would try to find the various elements of the power that was embedded in Sprite Towers.

It sounds as if Margaret Sprite was a clever woman and had extraordinary power, thought Flame. Perhaps she worked out that Sidney had hidden the magic somewhere in the house. She would have told *her* daughter, and she would have told her daughter – Glenda Glass, our sworn enemy.

Flame smiled a bitter smile as she remembered how Glenda was desperate to get hold of the magic box and plan. She had used Charles Smythson as her spy – but we thwarted him and kept it safe, she thought. With the aid of the plan, we opened the portal in the tower. How amazing was that! The Sprites have the ability to move back and forward in time. What a power that is!

But the dark side of the Sprite family, those people who used their power against others, were soon on our heels. Flame's jaw tightened as she thought about the ghost roaming Sprite Towers. Is it looking for the plan? Is the plan safe in my room? What happens if it steals it today, while I'm at school? Damn and blast, she thought. I should have brought it with me!

And her heart began to pound.

I've hidden the plan behind a book on my shelves, she thought, her palms moistening. The ghost will find it – and then what? And there's nothing I can do until I get home this afternoon . . .

In the seat across from her, in the back of the car, Ash turned. 'What's the matter?'

'George's plan,' whispered Flame, with a frown.

'Ah,' said Ash, quietly. Then she whispered, 'I am sure it will be safe. The ghost may be more interested in taking things like pens and cufflinks.'

'What about Archie – do you think he is safe?' whispered Flame.

'Oh, don't say that!' Ash looked horrified. 'Don't drum that up!'

Flame's tension did not abate, however. It was a day of mixed emotions. First, she saw Verena and Quinn standing close together as they talked in the Quad. Verena was smiling up at him with her beautiful blue eyes – and Quinn was smiling down at her.

Quinn McIver was a year older than her, with dark hair and dark, bright eyes. Flame thought the son of her parents' friends – the brother of Janey, Marina's best friend – was absolutely gorgeous. And she thought *he* thought the same about her. But – yet again – it looked as if he also liked Verena Glass.

Flame growled inwardly, but her feeling of outrage – *How could he, the rat!* – was instantly mixed with self-doubt. But of course he likes Verena, she thought, in an agony of mortification. *All* the boys like Verena . . . but he told me he really liked me! I'm never going to speak to him again . . .

Her mood lifted when she saw Mrs Lax, the sports teacher, who told her that she'd chosen Flame as captain of the girls' under-14 hockey team. Verena was to be her deputy. Hurrah, thought Flame, almost skipping with delight across the Quad.

A few minutes later, she was brought down to earth with a crash when Verena came up beside her as she walked to the science labs for their physics lesson.

'Well done on the captaincy,' said Verena, flicking back her long blond hair.

'Thank you,' said Flame. 'Well done being deputy.' What

was coming next, she wondered. Things were never straight-forward when Verena came to speak with her.

Verena glanced sideways at Flame. 'My grandmother told me an interesting story about Sprite Towers.'

'Oh?' said Flame.

'Did you know my family owned Sprite Towers before your family?' asked Verena, flicking back her hair again.

'I know that they owned an older house and the land – and that my great-great-grandfather, Sidney, bought it from your great-great-grandparents to build Sprite Towers,' replied Flame, her cheeks beginning to flush. There was no one better at winding her up than Verena Glass. Keep cool, she thought, keep cool . . .

'My great-great-grandmother died a poor woman,' said Verena, glancing briefly at Flame. 'Sidney knocked down her house and built himself a mansion. My grandmother says he did not help her, when he could have done.'

Flame stopped and turned. 'That's not true! That's not true at all!'

Verena smirked and kept walking. 'Well, you would say that, wouldn't you.'

Flame stood aghast, as her friend Pia came up beside her. 'Don't take any notice,' said Pia, who had seen the confrontation. 'You know what Verena is like.'

Flame looked at her friend's warm, dark eyes and smiled. 'Yes,' she said slowly. 'But why does she do it?'

'Because she likes the attention, and you're terribly easy to wind up,' said Pia, with a big smile.

Flame laughed.

'Come on now,' said Pia. 'Fantastic news about the hockey – well done!'

The conversation with Verena left a sour taste in Flame's mouth. All day, it preyed on her mind. Nothing upset Flame Sprite more than dishonesty. She knew, in her heart, that it was not Verena's fault that she did not know the real story, as her grandmother would have only told her one side of it.

Nonetheless, Flame was offended. It's outrageous for Verena to insinuate that Sidney deliberately hurt his sister, she thought. It was Margaret's dark magic that was the reason for Sidney's anger, not his lack of kindness! But how can I explain without telling her about Sprite magic? That beastly grandmother of hers is trying to get at us again . . .

At Sprite Towers, things were similarly confusing.

At one o'clock, Dad came out of his office and pottered through to the kitchen to make a sandwich for his lunch. He turned on the radio, then got out one of Mum's homemade loaves from the bread bin and put it on the board. Humming happily to himself, he went over to the fridge and took out some cheese, spring onions and tomatoes. Then he went to the pantry and got a jar of Grandma's chutney.

He was in a good mood. The engineers had almost finished and he'd got an interesting new architectural commission, which he was pleased about. Clutching the bread knife, Dad cut two thick slices and laid them on the board beside the loaf. Mum and Grandma would be in for lunch any minute.

He was just about to butter the slices when an icy shiver

ran all the way down his back. 'Urgh,' he shuddered.

At the same time, little Archie yelped. Dad looked down, and saw the puppy's hair standing on end.

Suddenly, as if from nowhere, a black swirling shadow whooshed across the room, right past his face. He gasped, turned, and saw a thin white hand come out of the shadow. It picked up the loaf of bread – and hurled it right across the huge kitchen.

Dad stood completely still. His heart pounded. All colour drained from his face.

As Mum and Grandma came through the hallway door, they saw him standing white as a sheet, holding the bread knife in mid-air, his mouth slightly open.

'Colin!' cried Mum, alarmed that he was unwell. 'What's happened? Here, sit down.'

She led Dad to a chair. He sat down, speechless, breathing heavily.

Grandma looked down at Archie. 'Look at Archie's coat,' she murmured.

'It's standing on end!' said Mum.

'The loaf . . .' said Dad, quietly.

Mum shivered and looked around the room. 'It's very cold in here.'

Dad pointed to the sink, silent.

Grandma walked to the sink, fished out the now wet loaf – and held it up.

Mum laughed sharply. 'Colin, why on earth is the loaf in the sink?'

Dad sighed, then said very quietly and deliberately,

'Something picked it up and threw it in there – right under my nose.'

Mum stared at him as if he was mad. 'What sort of "something"?'

'*It might sound ridiculous, but I can assure you it's what happened!*' said Dad, his voice tense. 'I'm not in the habit of wasting your homemade bread!'

Mum blinked in surprise. They were all silent.

Archie settled down into his basket with a little whimper.

Grandma turned to prepare some lunch. A few minutes later, they sat down at the table.

Grandma chewed thoughtfully. Shall I tell Ottalie and Colin about the girls' experience in the attics last night? she wondered. No, I think it will really frighten them, she decided.

'Have either of you seen my spectacles?' asked Mum, as she cut a slice of cheese. 'I was sure I'd put them down on the piano – but they're not there.' She laughed, feeling foolish. 'Maybe I put them somewhere else.'

Dad raised his left eyebrow and smiled wryly. 'My cufflinks, Ma's pen and now your spectacles. Whatever this "something" is, it seems to like moving our stuff about.'

'A flying loaf is pretty dramatic,' said Mum.

They concentrated on eating for a while, then Mum said, 'Marilyn, what do *you* think it is?'

Grandma looked steadily at her daughter-in-law. 'I think we may have a ghost in the house – and that it's somehow connected to what's happening outside.'

'The water, you mean?'

'The drilling of the well.'

'How would that create a ghost?'

'You think we've disturbed something,' said Dad, quietly.

Grandma nodded. 'The well is on the site of the old house. I think it must be some kind of unhappy spirit that's been released from the ground.'

Mum sighed. 'I'm not one to believe in ghosts. I always thought they were a lot of mumbo-jumbo.'

She looked at Dad. He shrugged, then said, 'So did I till this started.'

'What about you, Marilyn?' asked Mum. 'Do you honestly believe in ghosts?'

Grandma looked at her daughter-in-law with clear green eyes. 'I believe we should never underestimate the power of things we cannot necessarily see or measure.'

Mum looked back, thoughtfully. She loved her mother-in-law, and appreciated her strength and wisdom. 'So you do think it could be real?'

'Yes.'

Mum nodded, and considered Grandma's words. Dad stared into space.

Then Mum said, 'Okay, well, how can we get rid of it? Whatever it is, it's horrible having it here. I saw how it affected Colin and little Archie. Do you think it will disappear again when the engineers finish?'

Grandma shrugged. 'I don't think that will make any difference. It's out here now.'

Dad drew himself up. 'So you think it's something to do with the old house, Ma?'

'Yes,' said Grandma – and she told them the story of

Margaret and Sidney, without the magic bits.

Then Dad said, 'Sounds plausible to me.'

'If I believed in ghosts, it would seem to fit with what's happened,' agreed Mum.

Dad sighed loudly. 'So we have the vengeful spirit of Sidney's sister running around the house . . . Terrific.'

'I don't think we should be beaten by a ghost, however scary it is,' said Mum.

'That's the spirit,' said Dad.

'Nice pun, Colin,' laughed Mum.

Grandma looked worried. 'I'm off to France tomorrow, but I'm reluctant to leave you with this going on. I think I should postpone my trip.'

'But you can't let your friend down, Ma – you said you'd take care of her after her operation!' said Dad. 'She needs your help.'

Grandma sighed. She thought of the events of the night before with her granddaughters. Then she thought of her friend Susan, alone and needing her care. What should she do?

'Besides, we have to find a way to get your missing money back from Glenda,' said Dad. 'Susan had some new photos which may identify Glenda. You'll have a chance to talk to the police while you're out there.'

'Marilyn, you must go to France,' said Mum, leaning forward and touching her arm. 'We'll be fine here. Nothing awful is going to happen – we've only had a loaf fly across the kitchen and a few things go missing. As Colin says, Susan needs your care and attention – and she's a very old, dear friend. Besides, it'll do you good to get away and have a holiday.'

'God knows where that venomous woman, Glenda Glass, has hidden our family money,' said Dad, stabbing a piece of tomato with his fork. 'I'd like to see her put away for years.'

'Me, too,' said Grandma with a grim smile.

When they finished eating, Mum put on the kettle to make the engineers some tea. Dad went down the garden to talk to Charlie, the foreman.

Ten minutes later, he came back in and took the tray of hot tea from Mum.

'Charlie says the water level has dropped and the well will be finished on Monday afternoon.'

'That's good news,' said Mum.

'What about the tap for the new water supply?' asked Grandma.

'Charlie's got a plumber coming in to do that on Monday,' said Dad.

'Well, I'm glad we'll be straight again so soon,' said Mum. 'Now I must find my spectacles – I've got to give a piano lesson in ten minutes . . .'

And off she went to the dining room.

As soon as Flame got back from school, she rushed up to her bedroom. Ash followed her. Wondering what was going on, Marina and Ariel ran up behind them.

'What's happening?' asked Ariel, as they pounded up the stairs.

'The plan!' shouted Ash.

In her bedroom, Flame kneeled down in front of the bookcase and pulled out several large books from the bottom shelf. There was the small wooden box that contained the secret plan.

'Oh, thank God!' she said, opening the box to check the plan was inside. 'They're both here – the plan and George's letter.'

Ash, Marina and Ariel flopped down beside her.

'But how are we going to keep them safe?' asked Ash. 'We daren't leave them here. Sidney built an invisible hole in the wall to keep the letter hidden from Margaret. Hiding it on a bookshelf is not going to stop her for long.'

Flame looked at her sister. 'I'll have to carry them about – like I did when Charles was here.'

'But what will you do at games?' asked Marina. 'You can't carry them on you as you run up and down a hockey pitch!'

Flame chewed her lip. 'The ghost is in the house. I think it's safe at school.'

'Put them in your locker then,' said Ash.

'I'll have to,' replied Flame. 'Though I don't like the idea of letting them out of my sight.'

Ariel looked around the bedroom, her eyes wide as saucers. 'She might be in here now – watching us. She might have heard everything that we have said.'

The Sprite Sisters looked around the room, their hearts beginning to beat harder.

'She might come and snatch the plan from your hand,' said Ariel, her lip trembling.

Flame gulped. She opened the box, drew out the plan and

the letter, safely sealed in an envelope, and tucked them into her bra. 'They'll be safe here,' she said.

'Well, don't leave them out for the washing pile, like I did with George's letter,' smiled Ash.

'I promise I won't do that,' grinned Flame.

'We've got a ghost in this house,' announced Ariel, at the supper table.

Mum and Dad glanced at one another in surprise.

'Perhaps,' replied Mum. 'But it's nothing to worry about.'

'How do you know that?' asked Ariel. 'It might be a very nasty ghost.'

Dad smiled. 'I think it's more of a "funny" type of ghost. It threw a loaf of bread right across the kitchen at lunchtime – it landed in the sink.'

The Sprite Sisters looked astonished.

'Colin!' said Mum, sharply.

Dad looked at her. 'Well, it's better that they know, Ottalie.'

'It's okay – we've seen the ghost,' said Marina.

'When?' asked Mum.

'Last night in the dressing-up room,' said Marina, nonchalantly. 'It held up Grandma's old hat in front of Ariel and me.'

'It wiggled the hat about – and the air went all cold,' said Ariel. 'I felt like ice.'

'*What!*' said Mum. 'You didn't say anything!'

Flame groaned. She stared hard at Ariel, as if to say, 'Shut up!'

But it was too late. Ariel could not resist telling their parents.

'The hat moved out of the room – just sort of floated off – and along the corridor. We followed it up to the tower. But when we got up there, it had vanished. *Booph* – gone – just like that!'

Mum and Dad looked aghast.

'So where is it now?' asked Dad.

Ash shrugged. 'In another dimension?'

Mum looked at Grandma, her face tense. 'Did you know about this, Marilyn?'

Grandma looked back steadily, 'Yes, dear.'

'Why didn't you say something, after what happened at lunchtime?' said Mum, her voice rising.

'I thought it might worry you even more,' replied Grandma, calmly.

'Yes – you're right! It does worry me! It worries me a lot!' And Mum jumped up and rushed out of the room.

Dad swallowed hard. 'Er – I think your mother's a bit upset, girls.' He started to get up, but Grandma put out her hand and said firmly, 'It's okay, Colin, I'll go.'

And she followed Mum out of the kitchen.

Flame turned to Ariel, her face red with anger. 'Sometimes you are so stupid, Ariel!'

'You shouldn't have said anything,' said Ash, shaking her head.

Ariel began to cry.

'And I wish you'd just keep your trap shut sometimes, too!' Flame spat at Marina.

'I didn't mean to upset anyone!' said Marina, bursting into tears.

Flame glared. 'Yes, but you made it all sound such a laugh

– and really you were terrified! We all were!'

Dad put down his knife and fork. 'Hey, girls, *that's enough*,' he said, very firmly. 'Everyone's getting a bit over-wrought. Just calm down, please.'

They ate silently for a few minutes, then Grandma and Mum walked back into the kitchen. There were streaks of tears on Mum's face. 'Sorry,' she said, as she sat down. Dad and the girls looked at her anxiously. They rarely ever saw their mother cry.

Ariel whimpered. 'I'm sorry, Mummy.'

Mum leaned over and stroked her hair. 'It's okay. I'm glad you told me. I'd rather know.'

They waited as Mum settled down. Then she said, 'This is all a bit strange. I don't know anything about ghosts – I've never had to deal with one before. And so much has happened this week with the puppy, the water and all these people working in the garden.'

She looked around at her daughters, saw their anxious faces, then smiled. 'But I'm sure we'll all be okay. We Sprites are a tough lot.'

She smiled at Dad and the atmosphere at the table relaxed.

'Are we still going to have the Hallowe'en party, Mummy?' Ariel said through a mouthful of food.

Mum looked at Dad. 'What do you think?'

Dad nodded. 'Yes, let's keep things as normal as possible.'

'In that case, I think I should stay and help you,' Grandma said to Mum. 'You've so much to do with Archie and everything.'

'No, Ma,' replied Ottalie. 'You must go to France! We'll

be fine. The girls will help – and the water work has nearly finished.'

After supper, the Sprite Sisters went early to bed. As soon as they were in their rooms, they used their magic powers to protect the space, as Grandma had told them. They each made an invisible barrier across the door and windows, which would prevent anything harmful coming into their rooms.

Flame used her power of Fire to create a screen of white-hot flames, which would vaporise the cold energy of a ghost that might try to pass through. Marina used her power of Water to suck out the damp energy of the ghost and dessicate it to powder, should it try to cross her invisible barrier. With her power of Earth, Ash created a binding spell, so that the ghost would stick to her barrier and be trapped there.

Ariel stood in her bedroom and screwed up her ski-jump nose. How best to use her magic power of Air, she wondered. Should she create a wind that would blow the ghost back, away from the door? Or perhaps lift it up, high above Sprite Towers? No, I'll create a wind like a tornado, to spin the ghost behind my barrier. That should give it a good headache – if ghosts get headaches, she mused.

As they lay reading in their beds, each Sprite sister found herself looking up from her book, from time to time. Their magic was strong, but this was the first time they had used their powers in this way – and this ghost was unpredictable. But all was well that evening. In each bedroom, the air was calm and the sisters drifted off to sleep

* * *

Later, Mum and Dad settled the animals and locked the doors. Then Dad switched out the lights in the kitchen and they walked through the hall to the wide mahogany staircase.

'Goodnight, Sidney,' they both said, as they passed by the portrait of Sidney Sprite – it was family tradition that everyone did this as they went up to bed.

'I wonder if he sees the ghost?' mused Dad.

Mum laughed. 'Ariel says that Sidney sees everything.'

Dad chuckled. 'At the rate we're going, I might just start to believe her. By the way, did you find your specs?'

Mum screwed up her face. 'You'll never believe where they were. In the tower! Your mother suggested I go and look there. Well, I know I didn't leave them there.'

Dad sighed. 'Well, I hope nothing else goes missing. Can't say I like sharing the house with a light-fingered ghost.'

At the top of the banisters, he turned to look down to the hallway. All was still.

'Come on, love,' said Mum, gently. 'Everyone is safe.'

CHAPTER SEVEN

THE VISITOR

THE NIGHT passed peacefully. Everyone was up early on Saturday morning, as Dad was to drive Grandma to the airport.

The Sprites ate a hearty breakfast together, then Grandma went up to her room to finish packing her suitcase.

Flame sat on her bed, watching her. They were very close and Flame knew she would miss her while she was away.

'All quiet last night, then,' said Grandma, as she folded a shirt.

'Thank heavens,' said Flame. 'Perhaps the ghost has gone.'

'Let's hope so.'

Then Dad carried Grandma's case down to the car. Ash picked up Archie from his basket and they all went out to the driveway.

Bert looked very doleful, so Marina picked him up and made a fuss of him. Dad put the case in the back of the car and got in, while Grandma kissed Mum and her grand-daughters goodbye. Then she gave Bert a big kiss and stroked his long silky ears.

'I shall only be away a week,' she said. Bert did not look convinced, however.

As Grandma climbed into the car, Dad shouted through the open window, 'Girls, we'll start to build the bonfire when I get back!'

'Okay, Dad!' they all shouted. Then, waving away, 'Bye Grandma, have a lovely trip!'

'Give our love to Susan!' shouted Mum.

Mum and the four sisters watched as the big red car pulled away down the long drive.

Flame watched the longest, a thoughtful look on her face.

As they turned to go back into the house, Ariel looked up at Mum. 'A Hallowe'en party and a bonfire party in the same week – that's amazing!'

'Yes, you're lucky girls,' said Mum, putting her arm around Ariel's shoulder. 'The bonfire party's not really a "party" – just Stephen and Verena coming round – and Charles, if he comes up next weekend. But the Hallowe'en party, *that* will take some organising, especially as Grandma is not here to help.'

'We'll all help you, Mum,' said Ariel.

'Yes, don't worry, Mum,' added Ash.

'Two friends each, that's what you said,' said Marina.

'Yes, love,' smiled Mum. 'That'll be enough to cope with

in the middle of the school week.'

And they went back into the house.

In the kitchen, the sisters helped Mum to clear up. Archie bumbled around their feet and tried to chew the flaps on the girls' trainers.

'That puppy eats everything!' said Mum, looking down in disbelief.

'When shall we sort out the costumes for the party?' asked Flame.

'This afternoon,' said Mum. 'And your father wants to start making the bonfire.' She looked up at the big station clock, high on the kitchen wall. 'I've got to give a piano lesson in a few minutes. Now, girls, don't forget to tidy your bedrooms. Then there's the rabbit hutches – and your gerbils, Ariel.'

The doorbell rang. 'Okay, let's get on,' said Mum.

As Mum and her pupil went through to the dining room, the Sprite Sisters made their way up to their bedrooms. Flame, Marina and Ash walked up the staircase, but Ariel stopped at the bottom and looked at the portrait of Sidney Sprite. It was well-known in the family that Ariel talked to her great-great-grandfather.

As they rounded the banister on the first floor, her elder sisters looked down and noticed that Ariel was beckoning to them, furiously. '*Come here! Come back down!*'

Flame, Marina and Ash ran back down the stairs.

'What it is?' asked Ash, as they crowded round.

Sidney Sprite's jolly, whiskery face beamed out of the

portrait. Ariel was busily chatting, then listening. Her sisters waited – only Ariel could hear what her great-great-grandfather was saying.

Ariel nodded her head up and down, her mouth open wide in a look of astonishment. 'Okay, thank you, Sidney. Goodbye for now,' she said and turned to her sisters.

'Well?' asked Marina.

Ariel took a deep breath. 'He says we have to go straight away to the West Tower – that we're to have a visitor!'

'Is it the ghost?' asked Ash.

Ariel shook her head. 'No – it's someone we've been wanting to meet.'

'Whoever could it be?' asked Ash.

'Gawd knows,' said Flame.

'Well, *come on*, then!' said Marina and they charged up the stairs.

A few seconds later, the four girls burst into the West Tower. Bright October morning light streamed in through the high windows.

'There's no one here,' said Marina, looking round.

Flame stood in the middle of the wooden floor. 'Wait . . . I can feel something.' She turned slowly in a circle. Then she said, 'Let's stand in our four directions.'

Flame moved to the east wall and stood with her back against the cold bricks. Marina moved to the south wall, Ash to the west and Ariel to the north.

'Close your eyes,' said Flame, softly. Then, after a few seconds, 'Make the Circle of Power.'

As the four sisters focused their minds, a bright blue light began to run in a circle between them. Brighter and brighter and bigger and bigger the light grew – until it filled the room.

Flame opened her eyes – and gasped. In front of them were the rainbow light and the steps that led to the portal, which they'd seen only a few weeks ago.

Marina and Ash started.

Ariel gave a little scream. 'The portal!'

Then, down the steps came a tall, young man wearing the army uniform of a soldier in the First World War. As he stepped into the room, the girls could see that the top of his blond hair hung down a little way in the fashion of the day; the sides and back were cropped short. His eyes were bright blue, like Marina's. His face was handsome and kind.

'Oh my goodness!' exclaimed Flame, stepping forward.

'Blimey!' squeaked Ariel.

'It's *you*!' said Ash. 'The man in the portrait!'

'George!' cried Marina.

The young man turned to look at each of the girls and smiled.

'George Sprite!' exclaimed Flame, her face all astonishment. Here, in front of her was Sidney Sprite's son, whose portrait hung on the wall on the staircase, and whose letter Ash had found.

George nodded politely. 'Miss Flame Sprite, I presume,' he said and held out his hand. For a second, Flame stared at it. Then she held out her hand. Their hands met – and clasped in a firm handshake.

'But, how?' she said, her voice trailing to a whisper. 'You're not a ghost . . .'

George smiled. 'You created the Circle of Power and I came through the portal. I have come through time.'

'So you're *real*?' asked Ash, wide-eyed.

'Yes,' he nodded. 'I *am* real – but I do not have long here, so we must be quick.'

He turned to introduce himself to Marina, Ash and Ariel, who stood amazed. One by one, he shook their hands.

Ariel was speechless. George smiled down at the small, blond sister. 'Do you remember I carried you out of the portal?' he asked.

'Yes!' she burst out. 'I was *so* scared!'

'Thank you for saving Ariel,' said Flame. 'We thought we had lost her.'

George made a slight bow of his head. 'I was pleased to be of help. We Sprites must stick together.'

'You look just like your portrait,' said Ash, shyly.

'Well, that's a relief!' laughed George.

'You really *are* real, aren't you?' said Marina, as she shook his hand.

'Yes, I'm real, Marina,' said George.

Ariel blurted out, 'So, what is it you have to tell us? Sidney said it was important!'

George nodded. 'I must tell you about the ghost in the house.'

'We think it's Margaret Sprite!' exclaimed Ariel. 'And she's meant to be a *horrible* woman!'

'Yes, it is Margaret,' said George.

'Why has she come?' asked Flame. 'And how is she here?'

George looked at the sisters with a steady gaze, then he

said in a deep, clear voice, 'It was said that Margaret was heart-broken when she died. She had never got over losing her home and she blamed Sidney for taking it. We know he didn't, of course, but Margaret believed this and she became a very bitter woman. When she died her ghost returned here, to her old house, and found its way into the remains of the cellar. There it stayed, undisturbed and hidden below the lawn of Sprite Towers. Then, as the water began to rise under the lawn, it moved Margaret's spirit. When the engineers began to drill the well and opened the ground, they unwittingly released the ghost.'

'Grandma told us that Dad saw something come out of the hole in the lawn,' said Flame. 'He said it was like a whirling shadow. Apparently, the workmen saw it, too.'

'Margaret's ghost came into the house,' said Ariel, her eyes wide. 'And she's been stealing things – and she *really* frightened Marina and me the other night!'

'She scared our little puppy,' said Ash. 'And she threw a loaf of bread across the kitchen, which freaked out Dad.'

George nodded. 'So far she hasn't done any damage.'

Flame blinked in surprise. 'But you think she may?'

'Possibly. Margaret was a very unpredictable woman.'

'But what does she want?'

George held her gaze. 'She wants her house back.'

'What about the secret plan? Does she want that?'

'I don't think so – but there's someone else who does.'

Flame gulped. 'Glenda?'

George nodded.

'Oh no, not again,' said Ash, quietly.

George looked round at the sisters. 'Glenda Glass has used her magic power to contact the ghost of Margaret.'

'How do you know?' asked Flame.

'Because I have magic power that allows me to see the family future,' he replied, looking her in the eye.

'Will you tell us our future?' piped up Ariel.

George smiled down at her. 'No, Ariel, you have to find that out for yourselves. But I will try to guide you, if you are in danger.'

Marina stepped forward. 'Can you tell us what Glenda wants Margaret to do?'

George nodded. 'First, Glenda wants her to get the plan.'

'I have the plan and letter here,' said Flame, patting her chest. 'I'm keeping them with me all the time.'

'That's good,' said George. 'As long as the plan is close and you have used your power to protect you, Margaret won't be able to get it, as she won't be able to break through that shield of protection. But it has to be close and protected. Margaret has strong magic – and she will wait for you to get distracted. And Glenda is using her magic to watch you, too – so take care.'

Flame exhaled. 'I understand.' Then she turned away, pulled out the envelope from her T-shirt and handed it to George. He looked down at the thick cream paper with its elegant black handwriting.

They were all quiet for a moment, then Ash asked, 'George, how did you know we would find your letter?'

'My father and I had strong magic,' he replied. 'Some members of the Sprite family were beginning to use very dark magic. Father and I knew we had to protect the good magic in the family. We saw in our minds that you sisters would live here, at Sprite Towers, in the future. We knew that your magic would be good and true. I hid the letter at the back of my mother's portrait and put some strong magic around it, so that you would find it one day.'

'And we did!' giggled Ariel.

'Yes, you did,' George laughed. He pulled out the letter and the plan from the envelope, then handed the letter to Flame. Carefully, he unfolded the plan as the girls crowded closer.

On the old, thick white paper were drawn the floor plans of the four storeys of Sprite Towers. All over these were numbers, marks and scribbles drawn in black ink. Symbols and lines flashed in all directions.

George breathed out long and hard. 'There is a lot of magic in this plan,' he said, softly.

'We used it to open the portal,' said Flame. She pointed to the east side of the house marked on the plan. 'See – I stood here. Then, Marina stood at the south, here. Ash stood at the west – and Ariel stood at the north. When we stood like this and focused our minds, we found we could create this amazing blue light. We did this on all the floors of the house, starting at the ground floor and working our way up to the top. By the time we got to the towers, the blue light was incredibly strong – and the portal opened in front of us. As you know, Ariel stepped too close and got drawn in. Charles Smythson was spying on us for Glenda – and he got pulled in too. Thankfully, you brought them both out again.'

'I remember,' he said.

Flame pointed to the plan again. 'George, is *this* the secret to Sprite Towers? Grandma said there was something else.'

'This plan is *part* of the secret of the magic that my grandmother, Lily, passed to my father, Sidney Sprite,' replied George. 'Our family magic goes back a long, long way, but very few Sprites know about the other part of the secret. You girls will find it when you are ready. There are more elements to come into play, first. But for now, keep this away from Margaret's hands, or she'll take it for Glenda.'

Flame held his gaze, a thoughtful look on her face.

'And another thing,' said George, holding out the plan. 'Listen carefully. When these elements I have mentioned come into being, you will see the marks on the plan start to change – so keep a close eye on it. You will know what to do. There is more you have to learn.'

Flame nodded. Marina and Ash glanced at one another, wondering what he meant.

As George folded up the plan and handed it to Flame, Ariel piped up. 'Excuse me, George, but what do we *do* about Margaret's ghost? You say Glenda has got her to work for her. How are we to send her away?'

Flame, Marina and Ash drew breath.

George looked at the girls one by one and said, slowly, 'There is only one way to get rid of Margaret from Sprite Towers.'

The Sprite Sisters waited.

'You must go into the portal.'

'*What?*' squeaked Ariel. 'Oh no!'

Marina started. 'The portal?'

Flame's face went pale. 'Is that really the only way to stop her, George?'

'Yes,' he said.

'What do we *do* in the portal?' asked Ash.

'Go back in time and change the magic power around Margaret's spirit,' said George. 'You have to use the past to change the present. Only then will she leave Sprite Towers.'

'But not even Sidney Sprite could persuade Margaret to change her mind!' exclaimed Flame. 'How can we possibly do it?'

'It's because Margaret died bitter and consumed by her dark power that she has become a malevolent ghost,' said George. 'If you change her way of thinking in the past she will stop using her dark powers – and then she will leave Sprite Towers.'

Flame turned away and started to pace, anxiously, round the tower room. Marina gazed up at the high tower windows. Ash stared at the wall. Ariel stared at George.

Flame stopped and turned, her face dark with worry. 'I understand, George, but it's dangerous! You've travelled safely through the portal, but we don't know if Margaret might try to trap us. Or Glenda – she will stop at nothing!'

George breathed out slowly, then said in a measured voice, 'It is *your* choice, girls. I cannot define your future. But, if you want my guidance, I would say, "Use your powers to protect yourselves and go into the portal to meet with Margaret Sprite." There is no other way to stop her. Otherwise . . . she will take everything apart, bit by bit.'

'What do you mean?' asked Flame. 'Will she hurt us?'

'She has a dark magic power, Flame – and so does Glenda,' replied George. 'In order to protect the secret and keep Sprite Towers safe, you must get rid of Margaret's ghost. The combined dark power of Glenda and Margaret could grow too strong for you girls.'

They all stood, silent, for a while.

Then George said, quietly and firmly, 'If you decide to go into the portal, first get the measure of Margaret. You need to understand her. Don't go before you are ready – prepare first.'

The Sprite Sisters glanced at one another, then looked anxiously at George. A thoughtful look passed over his clear blue eyes. The sisters waited.

Then George looked at Flame and said, 'There's an object you need to find. It will help you to understand something that is part of the bigger "secret" – but it will also be of direct help with Margaret.'

Flame nodded and listened carefully.

'It will take some deep thinking on your part, Flame,' he continued. For a few seconds, he stared at the floor, then he said, 'I should wait until after Hallowe'en.'

Flame started. 'But I thought you said that her power and Glenda's would grow too much for us!' she exclaimed.

'Yes, it will – but you should have enough magic between you to protect yourselves for a short while. Don't rush, Flame.'

'Why can't you just tell us what it is, George?' piped up Ariel.

'Because you would not learn what you need to learn,' said George. 'You have to learn things for yourselves. It is only then that you fully understand what things mean.'

'Even if we're in grave danger?' asked Ariel.

'Sometimes, yes,' replied George, with a kind smile.

Ariel sighed. 'That's what Mrs Duggery says.'

'Well, she's right. If you have magic power, you have to be able to take responsibility for it.'

'I'm only nine!' said Ariel.

George smiled down at her. 'And that's why I am helping you.'

Marina caught George's gaze. 'Is *Margaret* making all that water on the lawn?'

'No, the water is a natural phenomenon,' said George, turning to her. 'Its movement provided Margaret with a means of escape.'

He looked around at the sisters, then up at the ceiling of the tower, a wistful look on his face. 'I must go now,' he said, quietly.

Flame bit her lip hard, then said quickly, 'Is the portal really the only way, George?'

'Yes, Flame.'

Ariel gave a low moan. 'The portal! Not again!'

Then Ash said, resolutely, 'We will go into the portal, George.' She looked round at Flame.

Her eldest sister smiled. 'Yes – and thank you for coming to help us.'

'Yes, thank you,' echoed Marina, Ash and Ariel.

George made a small, old-fashioned bow. 'You are most

welcome, Sprite Sisters. Good luck!'

'Goodbye!' whispered Ariel.

George walked to the middle of the floor and closed his eyes. The four Sprite Sisters walked to their positions around the tower wall. Flame stood at the east; Marina stood at the south. Ash stood to the west, facing Flame, while Ariel took the position of the north, opposite Marina.

'Close your eyes,' said Flame. As they closed their eyes, she announced, 'We come together as the Circle of Power.'

Immediately, a bright blue light began to glow in the middle of the room, around George. Brighter and brighter it shone, until he was enclosed in a huge ball of rainbow light. Once again, the steps appeared in the middle of the floor. George began to climb towards the portal.

How long the Sprite Sisters stood there, they did not know. In the Circle of Power, they had no sense of time. As the light glowed brilliantly, the Sprite Sisters felt an over-whelming sense of peace and happiness – and a sense of strength.

And, when they opened their eyes and looked around, George Sprite was gone.

For a moment they looked around the room. Then, silently, they sat down on the floor. Each was thoughtful, daunted by the task ahead.

Eventually, Marina said, 'When shall we go?'

'Tonight?' suggested Ariel.

Flame shook her head. 'No – not yet. George said to wait till after Hallowe'en. He said we had to find something first.'

'And to get the measure of this ghost,' added Ash.

'Will we make the Circle of Power in the portal?' said Ariel.

'Possibly,' said Flame. 'I've a hunch there is something we need to take with us.'

'Is this one of your "feelings"?' asked Ash.

Flame smiled. 'I need to think about it.'

'We must watch Margaret,' said Marina. 'And listen.'

Flame nodded thoughtfully. 'And guard the plan carefully.'

'Do you think we'll see George in the portal?' asked Ariel. 'He's so handsome!'

Flame laughed, then looked at her watch. 'Oh my goodness – come on! We've been here ages. Mum will have a fit. We were meant to do our rooms and clean out the animals.'

And they ran downstairs as fast as they could.

CHAPTER EIGHT

HALLOWE'EN PREPARATIONS

SUNDAY WAS a busy day. After breakfast, Dad and Ash picked the pumpkins in the vegetable garden and wheeled them, one by one, to the house in the barrow. Marina and Ash then started to hollow them out – which was a big job – while Mum made the week's bread and Flame made toffee apples and sticky gingerbread for the party.

On the table in the big kitchen, Ariel drew and cut out the shapes of skeleton bones on luminous white paper. As the bread baked, Mum helped her stick the pieces of paper to the back and front of a long-sleeved black T-shirt and a pair of black trousers. On a black balaclava, which Ariel had found in the dressing-up box, they stuck the shape of a toothy, grinning skull. When the costume was finished, Ariel put it on and 'haunted' the kitchen. Everybody laughed.

Mum was just helping Marina with her vampire costume, when Verena Glass rang the front door bell. Ariel ran to open it. Verena followed her into the kitchen, pale-faced and a little over-awed by the exuberant activity.

'Come in, Verena!' said Mum, and gave her a kiss. 'We're just getting ready for Hallowe'en.'

'I hope it's okay to come round,' said Verena, catching Flame's wary eye.

Mum put her arm around Verena's shoulder. 'Of course, dear! It's always lovely to see you. Marina said you'd be coming round and I know you wanted to have a chat with me. And please call me Ottalie – Mrs Sprite sounds far too formal.'

'Okay – thank you,' replied Verena, with a small smile.

'We're having a Hallowe'en party!' said Ariel, who now had bits of orange pumpkin flesh all over her skeleton outfit.

'And we'll be eating pumpkin soup until Christmas!' said Ash, rolling up her eyes and putting another handful of pumpkin into the saucepan beside her.

Verena joined in as best as she could, but found it hard with so much on her mind. As an only child, she did not find noisy families easy. Archie proved a good distraction, however. 'He's adorable,' she said, bending down to stroke him. 'I'd love to have a dog.'

Mum made some hot chocolate and handed Verena a cup. 'Let's go and have a chat in the conservatory,' she said, in her easy, motherly way. Verena grabbed her mug and followed.

While they were out of the kitchen, the Sprite Sisters carried on with their tasks. Flame was stirring the boiling toffee, which required concentration. Marina and Ash cut out the faces on their pumpkins. Ariel took off her costume and put on an apron, then began scraping out her pumpkin.

On the Aga, Flame gave the toffee a final stir and dropped a teaspoonful of the boiling liquid into a cup of cold water. She rolled it into a ball in her fingers – which meant it was ready. 'Perfect,' she said.

Beside the big pan, she had already laid out a tray of apples with sticks pushed into them. One by one, she twizzled the apples in the hot, sticky mixture and laid them on a dish to cool and harden.

Over at the table, Marina, Ash and Ariel were laughing. There was pumpkin everywhere. On the floor, Archie ate a small piece of orange flesh, then spat it out.

'I wonder where the ghost is today,' mused Marina, as she drew the eyes on her pumpkin.

'It's too warm and cheery in here for *her*,' said Ash, biting her lip with concentration, as she drew a jagged mouth on hers.

'Don't say that – you'll drum her up,' said Ariel, still scraping out her pumpkin.

Sure enough, a minute later, just as Mum and Verena walked back in, an icy blast suddenly swept through the kitchen. Everyone shuddered and stood still.

Mum looked around the room, an anxious look on her face. 'Oh no,' she murmured, softly.

'What is it?' asked Verena.

'*Look!*' Ariel shrieked, pointing at the pumpkins – which were now rising slowly in the air above the table, as if pulled by an invisible string.

Verena screamed. Flame, Marina and Ash gasped, their mouths open in astonishment.

'Oh my goodness!' said Mum, moving forwards.

The four huge orange spheres hovered in mid-air above the table. Everyone waited, silent and astonished.

Then, suddenly – *BANG!* – the pumpkins dropped down with a huge crash. The table juddered. Pumpkin flesh flew everywhere.

Verena screamed again. Mum clasped her hand over her mouth, her eyes wide. Marina, Ash and Ariel cried out. The hair on Archie's back stood up like bristles. Bert barked. Pudding, the cat, arched his back and hissed.

And Flame spun round, looking for the ghost. Where is she? *Where is she?* she wondered.

But there was nothing to be seen.

'It's okay, everybody – calm down!' shouted Mum above the mayhem.

'But what's happening?' cried Verena. 'Why did the pumpkins lift up like that?'

'GO AWAY!' shouted Ariel, into thin air.

'Who are you shouting at?' cried Verena.

'The ghost, of course!' said Ariel.

'*Ghost?*' Verena looked around the room in horror.

'*Ariel, be quiet!*' said Flame, sharply.

'That's *enough*, Ariel,' said Mum, very firmly.

Verena stood as if frozen.

Marina noticed Archie huddling under the table and picked him up.

For a moment they were all silent. There were bits of

pumpkin everywhere – all over the table and the floor around it.

Then Mum said in a no-nonsense voice, 'Come on, let's get this mess cleared up. Ariel, come and finish your pumpkin, love.'

Flame got a brush and dustpan and began to sweep up the floor. Ash, Marina and Verena picked up pumpkin flesh from the table. Ariel sat down with her knife and began scraping again.

When everything was cleared up, Mum put her arm around Verena's shoulder and said, in a matter-of-fact voice – as if this sort of thing happened every day at Sprite Towers, 'Verena, we seem to have a ghost that likes to joke about.'

'Oh,' said Verena, with a small smile.

Then Mum looked round at her daughters and said, 'Listen, girls – I've invited Verena to join us at the party on Wednesday.'

'Goodie!' said Marina and Ariel. Ash smiled her quiet smile. Verena smiled, then looked doubtful as Flame looked away.

'You'd better make a face on a pumpkin then,' said Marina, handing Verena a black felt pen and a small, sharp knife.

When Ash finished her pumpkin – which had slanting eyes and a wide zig zag of a mouth – she moved away from the chattering girls to speak with Flame, at the corner of the kitchen.

'Verena will be okay at the party,' she said, quietly.

Flame looked doubtful. 'But what will she tell that

grandmother of hers?' she whispered. 'And it will make thirteen of us, which I don't like. Thirteen is an unlucky number, and we don't want any bad luck before we go into the portal.'

Ash sighed. 'Hm, there is that. Still, nothing we can do now.'

'I wish Marina would stop being so flipping chummy with her.' Flame cast her sister an angry glance and caught Verena's eye.

Ash whispered, 'Verena's not all bad, Flame – and she's having a rotten time without her mum.'

'I know – and I'm sorry for that,' whispered Flame. 'But we still can't trust her – and it's *her* great-great-grandmother that's scaring us all witless in this house!' And she walked out of the kitchen and went up to her room.

Everyone noticed Flame's silent and sudden departure. Ash knew her sister well enough to understand how she felt.

Marina turned, wondering if she should follow Flame, but Mum said, 'Marina, why don't you take Verena up to the attics and see if you can find her an outfit for the party, before we have lunch.'

Verena's face lit up so much that Marina felt sad for her – touched at the thought that here was a girl who had beauty, intelligence and the sort of clothes and holidays the Sprite Sisters could only dream of, but no sisters or brothers to hang out with. As they climbed the stairs to the attics, Marina asked, 'Did you and Mum have a good chat?'

Verena nodded. 'Yes – and I feel so much better, thank you.' Then she said, 'I could hire an outfit for the party.'

Marina laughed. 'I expect you could, but it's much more fun to do your own. We're never allowed to hire anything.

Mum says it's a waste of money – and that we've enough dressing-up clothes to make whatever we need.'

But, as she climbed the stairs, Marina prayed the ghost would not make another call them in the dressing-up room.

In her room, Flame lay on her bed. As usual, her anger passed quickly and her mind moved on to solving problems. As the Sprite Sister who saw ahead, Flame often did much of the thinking and planning. The matter of the portal was pressing.

We need to be protected, thought Flame. We need to plan, to work out what Margaret might do, what we might need . . .

There was something touching the edge of her mind. For some while she lay there, staring at the ceiling, her mind whizzing and whirring. Then she sat up and pushed back her thick copper-coloured hair, her green eyes sharp, focused.

Using her power of the East, Flame used her imagination to look forward in time. She had the clear sense that there was something she needed to carry into the portal.

This object is something that will disempower Margaret, she thought, something that we hold up in front of her. What could it be?

Flame stared at the ceiling. The word 'remember' flickered at the edge of her mind.

Was it something they had to remember?

Or was it Margaret? Was there something that she had to remember – something she had forgotten? What would make her 'remember'? A favourite object? A toy, a book, a photograph?

Flame got up off the bed, walked to the window and

looked out at the trees blowing in the wind. Autumn leaves were scattered everywhere. Then she looked out beyond the grounds, to the fields and up to the bright blue sky.

I'll find it, she thought. Now my mind is focused, whatever it is I need to find will come to me. But, as she walked out of her room, back down to the kitchen, the issue of time came into her mind – and it unsettled her. I know I *can* find this thing that I need, she thought, but can I do it in *time*? Where *is* this object? Where do I start?

After lunch, Marina, Verena, Ash and Ariel played with Archie, then raced their bicycles around the lawn, while Flame did some violin practice and finished preparing her Hallowe'en costume.

In the library, Mum and Dad sat by the fire, drinking coffee and reading the Sunday papers. Mum told Dad the gist of what Verena had told her that morning, and how unhappy she was living with Glenda.

'I'm not surprised,' he replied, putting down his newspaper. 'Glenda must be hell to live with, poor kid.'

'I'm very concerned,' said Mum, staring at the fire.

'Stephen and Zoe's marriage is not our business,' said Dad. 'What can we do?'

'Nothing – about the marriage – but we have some responsibility to Verena, and we ought to tell Stephen how unhappy she is with her grandmother,' said Mum, pushing back her wavy, blond hair.

She stared at the fire for a few seconds, then said, 'You know, I've never liked Glenda. Ever since we met her this summer, I've felt there's something odd about her. She's so rude – and you know how I feel about rudeness.'

Dad smiled wryly. 'Hm,' he agreed.

'And since your mother discovered that it's possibly Glenda who has stolen her inheritance – well, I just think the woman is the pits.'

'I wonder if I should say something to Glenda, when I take Verena home?' said Dad, rubbing his chin thoughtfully.

Mum gave a sharp laugh. 'It'll be water off a duck's back. She'll probably tell you to get lost!'

Dad smiled.

'I think we should speak to Stephen,' said Mum.

'Yes,' Dad agreed, rubbing his chin again. 'I'll give him a call this evening.'

Soon after this, the Sprite Sisters, Verena, Archie and Bert piled into the library and sat down by the fire.

'How's Bert getting on with Archie?' asked Dad. He leaned down to stroke the sleek brown sausage dog. 'How are you, mate? Are you bearing up with all these women and all this fuss?'

Bert raised his head and seemed to smile, man to man. Dad laughed.

'He's missing Grandma,' said Ash.

'Yes, I expect he is,' agreed Dad. 'She'll soon be back.'

As Archie was passed from girl to girl, Mum commented, 'It's a wonder Archie has any hair left on him, with all that stroking.'

'He may be going bald, but he loves the attention,' smiled Marina.

'He's *not* going bald!' objected Ariel.

'He peed on the kitchen floor again,' said Ash.

Mum gritted her teeth.

'We cleared it up,' said Ash, quickly.

'Thank you,' said Mum.

'So are all your costumes ready for the party, girls?' asked Dad.

'Yes,' said Flame.

'And everything quiet in the house?' said Dad.

'How do you mean?' asked Marina.

Dad grinned. 'You know – after the Flying Pumpkin Incident!'

Verena giggled.

'The FPI, you mean?' said Flame. 'Or should it be an FLI – a Flying Loaf Incident?'

Worried what Verena would think, Mum shot Dad a cross look. 'Colin – please! Don't stir things up.'

The Sprite Sisters laughed. 'Keep your hair on, Mum!' giggled Marina.

'It's all quiet, Dad,' said Ash. 'There's not so much as a carrot hovering over the kitchen table.'

Ariel cupped her hands around her mouth and announced in a mechanical voice, '*Zero FPI, I repeat, we have zero FPI to report. All clear in the kitchen!*'

Mum made a 'do you really have to' face, then smiled at Verena.

'What do you make of us all, Verena?' asked Dad. 'Do you think we're bonkers?'

Verena grinned. 'Only a little.'

Dad burst out laughing. 'Well, that *is* a relief! Glad we're only partly bonkers!'

A little while later, he said, 'Well, we'd better get you home, Verena. I'll put your bike in the car.'

'I'll come with you,' said Marina.

Sure enough, when Dad started to tell Glenda that he and Mum were concerned about Verena, he met with her iciest look. 'Thank you, Colin, and goodbye,' she said, closing the front door in his face. Behind him, Marina kicked the gravel.

Dad was silent as he got into the car and all the way back to Sprite Towers. From time to time, Marina looked at him, but said nothing.

That evening, Dad called Stephen Glass on his mobile phone. As a top City lawyer, he travelled often. Stephen greeted him, cheerily. 'Morning, Colin! I'm in Japan today. Just having breakfast!'

For a few minutes, Dad nattered to Stephen about work. Then he passed the phone to Mum, who told Stephen about Verena's visit and their conversation. Stephen listened, concerned, then told her he would call Verena and be up to see her as soon as he returned home next weekend. He was also delighted, he said – if Verena was right – about Zoe wanting to come home.

'That would be wonderful – for everyone,' agreed Mum. 'See you next weekend then.'

The only person who was not cheered by the day's happenings was Glenda Glass. The sight of Colin Sprite on the doorstep, hinting that Verena was unhappy, was enough to make her blood boil. Dark thoughts began to form in her mind. Those Sprites, she thought, those blasted Sprites . . .

For some minutes she walked restlessly around the big house. Verena has disappeared to her room, she thought, staring up the staircase. Well, I shall ask her over supper . . .

By suppertime, Verena hoped Glenda had cooled down, but her grandmother dived straight in. 'So what have you been telling the Sprites?' asked Glenda, her blue eyes cold as ice.

All Verena's feeling of comfort disappeared in an instant. Where were the kind family now, when she needed them? She stared at her grandmother with a sense of dread.

A battery of questions was coming, she knew. She was well aware how insistent her grandmother could be. I don't want to talk about Mummy, she thought. I don't want to let Grandma know what I really feel. How can I divert her attention? How can I stop her asking me questions? What can I say?

Just as Glenda was about to launch a volley, Verena pre-empted her, saying, quickly, 'There's a ghost at Sprite Towers!'

Glenda stopped, her fork held in mid-air. 'Really?'

'Yes! I saw it! Well, at least I saw what it *did*.'

'And what did it do?' Glenda's long fingers tightened around the handle of the fork.

'It lifted the pumpkins in the air!'

Glenda's cold blue eyes never left Verena's. 'And?'

'They came crashing down on the kitchen table!' Verena laughed, remembering. 'Ariel shouted at it.'

'It?'

'The ghost,' said Verena. 'First, though, the air went incredibly cold. It was so weird.'

Glenda smiled. In her mind, she had been using her power to connect with the ghost of her grandmother, Margaret. She had asked Margaret to scare the Sprites – and to get her the plan.

Verena began to relax. She is interested in this story, she thought. She is looking at me strangely.

'Who was in the kitchen?' asked Glenda.

'Mrs Sprite and the girls and me.'

'Where was the grandmother?'

'She's gone to the south of France,' said Verena, cutting a piece of potato.

Glenda was silent. The thought of Marilyn Sprite in France, possibly on the trail of her missing money, was unsettling, but the pumpkin story still had her attention. 'So were they all frightened?' she said, slicing her meat.

'Yes – we all were. It happened so quickly.'

Glenda raised an eyebrow.

'The puppy didn't like the ghost at all,' continued Verena. 'His coat stood up like prickles and he made a whiney noise.'

'What did Mrs Sprite do?'

'Oh, she told us to calm down. Then we had to clear up the mess. There was pumpkin everywhere, as the girls had been scraping them out. Oh yes – and Mrs Sprite invited me to their Hallowe'en party on Wednesday. I can go, can't I?'

Glenda ate silently.

'I've never seen a ghost before – not that I saw this one,' said Verena. 'But I did feel this incredibly cold air around me, when it whooshed up the pumpkins.'

'Then what happened?'

Verena shook her head. 'We had lunch, then went outside on our bikes. It was really good fun.'

Glenda was silent again.

'I can go to the party, can't I, Grandma?'

'Yes, dear – and you can tell me all about it afterwards. I shall be waiting to hear if the ghost makes another appearance. Now that would make for a real Hallowe'en.'

Verena looked at her grandmother anxiously. What is it she wants me to tell her? she thought.

Just then, the phone rang. 'It'll be Daddy,' said Verena, running to answer it before Glenda could.

'Daddy! I'm so pleased you've called! You'll never guess what's happened!' And she took the phone up to her room, shut the door and, for the next half hour, told him all her stories, particularly the one about her mother wanting to come home.

CHAPTER NINE

THE OPEN DOORS

ON MONDAY morning, the Sprite Sisters climbed into the big red car. As Mum drove them to school along the country lanes, Marina, Ash and Ariel chatted about the party, now only two days away. Flame stared out of the window silently, lost in thought.

Every so often, she patted George's plan and letter, which were tucked in the breast pocket of her school blazer. Still there. Must keep them safe, she thought.

Flame's thoughts turned to Margaret Sprite. I wondered what she looked like? I've seen Sidney and my great-great-grandmother Mim's portrait – but I don't think I've ever seen a picture or photograph of Margaret Sprite. She turned to her mother beside her. 'Have we got any really old photographs of the Sprite family, Mum?'

'How far back do you mean?'

'I was wondering if we'd any of Lily and Arthur and their children,' said Flame.

'I'm sure we have, somewhere.' Mum was silent for a few seconds as she changed down a gear to turn a corner, then said, 'I think Charles Smythson found some, which he was using to identify the portraits.'

'Has he taken them away?'

'No, I think he left them here,' said Mum. 'I expect he'll be up to see us at the weekend, as he's completed the inventory.'

'Charles is coming back,' murmured Flame. Can we trust him now? she wondered. Has he changed – or is he still Glenda Glass's spy? It's the last thing we need this week. We've enough to think about with the ghost, the portal and Grandma being away.

'So where are these photos?' asked Flame.

'There's a box somewhere,' replied Mum. 'Why do you want them?'

'I've got to think up a story for English and I'd like to do something on my family. Where will the box be?'

'Probably in the big cupboard in your father's office, but you know what a lot of clutter he has in there.'

Flame grinned. 'He's not like you, Mum. Your cupboards are neat and tidy. You'd chuck everything out, if you had the chance.'

Mum laughed. 'When you're grown up and have to keep Sprite Towers clean, you'll understand why!'

* * *

At Sprite Towers all was quiet that morning. Dad was making some early calls in his office at the back of the house. The engineers had not yet arrived. In the kitchen, Archie and Bert were asleep in their baskets, beside the warm Aga. Pudding was curled up on the Windsor chair. Throughout the huge house, the doors were closed – to keep the warm rooms warm and reduce any cold drafts.

But, as Mum dropped off the girls at Drysdale's School, the ghost of Margaret Sprite began to move through Sprite Towers. As Dad chatted on the phone, it began in the West Tower. And, as it moved down through the house, it opened every door and every window. Within a few minutes, windows rattled and doors banged, as the cool autumn wind blew through the house.

In his office, the door shut, Dad did not hear the windows rattling, or feel the icy drafts sweeping through the house.

It was Mum who saw something was wrong. As she came up the drive, she was thinking about what she had to do that day – but the sight of all the open windows and the open front door alarmed her. And there, on the gravel in front of the house, was Archie, wobbling about on his stubby little legs. Beside him, Bert was sniffing the gravel.

Mum pulled up hard and jumped out. Grabbing Archie and calling Bert, she ran in through the open front door. The hallway was freezing.

Mum spun around, saw that the drawing-room windows were open. '*COLIN!*' she shouted, at the top of her voice.

Dad had just finished a telephone call in the office. He jumped up from his seat, opened the door and walked quickly into the hall. Mum was standing there, holding Archie, her face tense and pale.

'Ottalie – what's the matter?' he asked.

'For heaven's sake – didn't you realise? The dogs were out on the drive and the front door wide open! It looks as if every window is open at the front of the house!'

'What?' said Dad, staring at her. 'But there's nobody here! Charlie and the men haven't arrived yet and I've been on the phone. I left the dogs in the kitchen!'

He walked to the dining room. A gust of cold autumnal air blasted through the room. He shivered slightly and pulled the windows shut.

Meanwhile, Mum walked through to the kitchen, shut the back door and put Archie in his basket. Dad walked through to the drawing room and shut the windows there.

'It doesn't look as if anything has been taken,' he said, as Mum came out of the kitchen. They walked through to the conservatory. The ornate glass doors were banging in the wind. As he shut the doors, the engineers drove on to the lawn. Mum and Dad gave them a wave.

'Burglars wouldn't open all the windows,' said Mum.

'And Charlie and his men have only just arrived, so it wasn't them,' said Dad. 'Come on, let's take a look upstairs.'

They walked quickly up the staircase. At the top of the landing, they stopped and looked round.

'It feels as if there's a howling gale blowing through the entire house!' exclaimed Dad. 'I reckon every blasted window *is* open!'

Mum grabbed his arm. 'Colin – if this isn't burglars, then

who or what has opened all the windows?'

'I don't know, love,' he said. 'It's very strange.'

On the first floor, every door was open in every room – even the wardrobe and cupboard doors. One by one, they closed them, then they walked up to the second floor. Every door was open there, too.

'This is weird,' said Mum.

Dad shook his head in disbelief as he looked along the corridor. They were both very quiet.

Then Mum said, 'I know what you're thinking. You think it's the ghost, don't you?'

Dad turned and looked at her. He rubbed his chin, a sure sign that he was troubled. He hesitated, then said, 'Well, love, I don't think any human being has done this.'

'Oh, for heaven's sake!'

'I know you don't believe in these things, Ottalie – but you *saw* the pumpkins move yesterday! And the girls saw the moving hat in the attic. And then I had a loaf of bread thrown across the room. It makes sense!'

Mum frowned.

'You can't honestly think someone's broken into the house to open the windows!' said Dad.

Mum looked at the carpet. 'No . . . you're right.' Then she looked around and continued, 'Well, how do we get rid of this thing?'

'I wish I knew,' said Dad, shutting Marina's wardrobe doors.

'What does it want?'

'It certainly seems to want us to know it's about – but

why, I don't know.'

'I wonder how much the girls are being affected,' said Mum, pulling down Marina's window.

'They're pretty resilient,' said Dad, as they walked into Ash's room.

'What about this party on Wednesday?' asked Mum. 'I wonder if we ought to cancel it.'

'And say what?' said Dad. 'That we're cancelling our Hallowe'en party as we have a real ghost? Everybody will think it's a joke!'

Mum nodded. 'Hm, you're right. But I do feel uneasy.'

Dad put his arm around her. 'Yes, I know you do, love. But listen – the ghost hasn't done any harm. It's annoying us, that's all.'

In the attics, every door was open wide. An icy wind cut through the air, as Dad and Mum walked quickly up the corridor and into each room. Then they shut the tower doors at either end – through which came piercingly cold blasts of air – and went back downstairs.

'What a *waste* of heat!' said Mum, her face drawn.

Dad's jaw clenched tight. 'I will *not* let this ghost stop us from living our lives.'

As they walked down to the kitchen, Mum said, 'Colin, let's not say anything about this to the girls.'

'No,' he agreed. 'And if it appears at the party, we'll say it's part of it – that it's some kind of trick.'

Mum put the kettle on the Aga and got out mugs and a tray. A few minutes later, when she had made the coffee, she opened the back door and called to Charlie.

The big, blustery foreman came in. 'Mornin',' he said in a slow Norfolk accent.

'Morning, Charlie,' Mum and Dad said together.

'Everythin' awright?'

Dad rubbed his chin and smiled. 'Well, Charlie, there's been some funny things happening here since we dug the well.'

Charlie nodded. 'Tol' yoo thar's a ghust here. Oi saw it come out that there hole. Was it dun now?'

'Opened all the doors and windows right through the house,' replied Dad.

Charlie gave a grim smile. 'Well blast me! Yoo better git rid'er that then.'

Dad smiled.

Then Mum said, 'Nearly finished then?'

Charlie nodded. 'Yep, plumber'll be here in a minute, then we're all dun.'

'That's wonderful,' said Dad.

'Don't let the coffee go cold,' said Mum.

'Roight ho then,' said Charlie, and he picked up the tray of mugs and carried it outside.

'I'll be out in a minute,' said Dad, shutting the door behind Charlie.

'Well, he didn't seem the least surprised about the ghost,' said Mum.

'He's a countryman, so he's bound to be superstitious,' said Dad. 'You were brought up in the city – a French city, at that. You don't believe in ghosts, but many people do, especially country folk.'

'You think I need to open my mind?' she smiled.

'Events would seem to point that way,' chuckled Dad.

'Well, how do we get rid of this – this – *ghost?*'

'Ottalie, I have no idea.'

'Just don't say anything to the girls,' said Mum.

That afternoon, as soon as Flame got home from school, she asked Dad to find the old photographs that Mum had referred to. Dad was vague about family history, and his office was a jumble.

'I thought architects were tidy people,' said Flame, gazing around at the higgledy-piggledy shelves of books, the wide chests crammed full of huge architectural plans and various bulging cupboards.

'I *am* tidy,' said Dad, opening a drawer.

'You're tidy in the garden,' said Flame, peering in. 'But not with all your "stuff", you're not. So where are our family photographs?'

'I'll find them,' said Dad, looking in a cupboard.

'They can't have gone far. Mum says Charles was looking at the photos a few weeks ago.'

'Yes, he was – but he left the box here,' said Dad, opening a drawer.

Five minutes later, he found the box of photographs at the back of a cupboard.

'Take care of these,' said Dad, handing the box to Flame.

'I will, I promise.' Flame's eyes were bright with excitement. She clutched the box to her and ran up the stairs two by two, to her room.

CHAPTER TEN

PUMPKIN EYES

AS DARKNESS fell, Flame sat on her bed looking at the old photographs. In the dining room, Mum was giving a piano lesson and Dad was making some calls in his office. Marina, Ash and Ariel sat at the kitchen table, doing their homework.

The girls worked quietly in the warm room. When they finished, Marina said, 'Let's light the pumpkins!'

'Okay,' agreed Ariel.

On the sideboard sat the four round pumpkins. Ash and Ariel lifted off the 'lids', while Marina struck a match and lit the nightlights nestling in the bottom of each hollowed-out pumpkin. When they were all lit, Marina said, 'Let's turn out the light, so we can really see them.'

Ash moved to the wall and flicked up the light switch.

Suddenly, the only light in the kitchen came from the four pumpkins, which glowed a beautiful orange. The backs of the pumpkins looked warm and comforting, but the faces were eerie. The cut-out shapes now glowing in the dark gave the pumpkins a crazy feel. Four mad, angry faces – with devilish eyes and crooked, jagged mouths – glowered back at the girls.

'Blimey, they look fierce!' said Ash.

'They're amazing!' laughed Marina, pointing. 'I like the mouth on your one.'

'I like the eyes on yours,' said Ariel.

'Look at the jagged mouth on Flame's pumpkin!' said Marina.

For a few moments they stood, watching the four glowing pumpkin faces, and all was still.

Then Ariel shivered. 'Oooh, I feel all goosebumpy, suddenly.'

'Me too,' said Ash, rubbing her hand on her arm.

Ariel looked around the kitchen, but there was nothing there.

Then Marina whispered, 'There's something very strange about those pumpkins.'

'Yes, I feel it, too,' whispered Ariel. 'It's almost as if they're alive.'

As she said this, an icy draft cut through the air. The three girls froze. Ariel let out a squeak of fear.

At the same time, Ash's magic stone emitted a loud *beep*. She pulled it out of her pocket and gazed at it in the dark, while Marina spun round quickly and looked up and down the dimly lit room. Under the table, Archie whimpered. Bert gave a little yowl.

After a moment's silence, Ariel spluttered, '*They're watching us!*'

Ash looked up from her magic stone. '*Who?*'

'*The eyes! Look!*'

'Of course they're watching us – they're faces!' said Marina, though she could feel the hair on the back of her neck stand up.

'No – they're *really* watching us!' exclaimed Ariel. '*There's something inside the pumpkins!*'

The three sisters stood transfixed, their hearts pounding.

Ariel moved a few steps to the right, away from the side-board. As she did so, the eyes inside the four pumpkins swivelled to the right.

Marina gasped. '*The eyes moved!*'

'They're following me,' whispered Ariel.

Marina stared in horror. 'You move, Ash – see if they follow you.'

Ash moved a few steps to the left, towards the hall door, all the time watching her own pumpkin. 'It's following me,' she whispered hoarsely.

The four pairs of eyes followed Ash.

'They're *all* watching you!' gasped Marina.

Ariel cried out, 'They're *horrible*! Blow them out!'

Ash rushed forward and grabbed one of the lids, as Marina moved towards the kitchen lights.

Ariel watched, shaking like a leaf. 'Turn on the lights,' she moaned.

'Don't say anything to Mum!' whispered Marina, flicking the switch on.

Ash had just finished putting the lid back on the last pumpkin when Mum walked through the kitchen door.

'Where's Flame?' she asked.

'In her room,' replied Marina, as calmly as she could.

Ariel stood, stock-still, in the middle of the kitchen.

'Ariel, are you okay?' asked Mum. 'You look very pale.'

Ariel nodded. 'Yes, yes,' she said quickly, turning away.

Thankfully, Mum was immediately in a 'busy' mode. 'Good – then set the table, please,' she said. 'Marina, make some salad dressing. Ash, call Flame down for supper – and get your father.'

As she opened the oven door on the Aga, a wonderful aroma of herby chicken casserole filled the kitchen. Suddenly, the kitchen was warm and bustling with movement. Ariel set the table and started chatting to her mother, Marina and Ash were busy with their tasks. Dad walked in and helped Mum lift the casserole and dishes of vegetables to the table, whilst Flame ran a jug of water at the tap.

At the table, the girls sat down and Mum began to serve up. Marina and Ariel looked over at the pumpkins on the sideboard. Ash, whispering, quickly explained to Flame what had happened with the pumpkin eyes. Flame looked amazed.

'It's gone now,' whispered Ash.

As he sat down, Dad looked round at the sideboard and said, 'I thought you'd have lit your pumpkins this evening, girls!'

The four Sprite Sisters started.

'We didn't want them to shrivel up before the party,' said Marina, with a forced smile.

Dad was soon distracted by his food. 'Delicious casserole, Ottalie,' he said, tucking in.

Across the table, Mum and Dad exchanged relieved glances. The doors and windows had stayed shut all day, and they would remain silent about their experience that morning.

The Sprite Sisters kept quiet about the pumpkin eyes. Everyone enjoyed their supper. From time to time, Flame looked around the kitchen. I wonder where Margaret is? she thought. She's in the house somewhere . . .

She caught Marina's eye, then Ash's, then Ariel's. They each glanced towards the sideboard, then relaxed as they saw all was still.

As they finished the main course, Dad said, 'Come on, girls – light your pumpkins! I'd love to see what those mad faces look like, all lit up. It won't shrivel them just to have a look for a few minutes.'

'Yes, I'd like to see them too,' added Mum. 'There's some matches over there.'

The Sprite Sisters looked at one another. What should they do?

Marina got up. 'Okay,' she said, in a tense voice. One by one, she lifted the lids and lit the nightlights.

'Just turn out the light, Marina,' said Mum.

Marina hesitated – then walked to the wall.

In the darkness, the orange faces glowed. The Sprite Sisters held their breath – but the eyes were still.

'Wow – they're amazing!' said Dad. 'What crazy faces!'

'Yes,' said Mum, smiling. 'Well done, girls!'

With a burst of relief, Marina turned on the light and said, 'Okay, that's it for this evening!' And she blew out the night-lights.

Dad laughed. 'Well, that was quick!'

A moment later, Mum got up to organise pudding, while Flame and Ash collected the plates and dishes. Dad leaned down to stroke Archie, who was sniffing about his feet.

'Hello, little chap,' he said.

As soon as supper was cleared up, Flame went to her room. Sitting in bed, under the bright red duvet to keep warm, she quickly became absorbed. In front of her was a notebook and pen in which she had scribbled various notes. Beside these, laid in neat piles on the duvet, were black and white photographs – dozens of them. And, in the box that Dad had given her, were a dozen more photographs she had yet to look at.

Flame loved history. As she gazed at the photographs, she saw stories – stories of love, achievement, failure, hope and friendship. To Flame these images of doe-eyed children, stern men with whiskered faces, dreamy women in dresses that buttoned right up their necks, weren't just people staring at the camera. They were her family. They were real.

They lived their lives as we are now living our lives, she thought. They felt happy and sad, like we do. They ached and cried and worked hard – and they had dreams, like we have dreams. And some of them walked the corridors of Sprite

Towers. Some of them played in the gardens. And one of them, she thought, staring at a photograph of George Sprite in his army uniform, went to war and didn't come back.

She laid the photograph on the bed, on the 'George' pile. Then she rested her chin in her hands and looked down at the pile she had earmarked as 'Sidney'. She stared at this for a few seconds, then put her hand into the box and drew out another photograph – this one quite small. It was the image of a blond-haired girl about fifteen years old, standing with two boys, one about the same age, the other a bit older.

One of these boys Flame recognised as George Sprite. The other seemed familiar. Ah yes, she thought, it's his elder brother Frederick – my great-grandfather. So who is the girl? she wondered. One of their sisters, I expect.

Flame stared at the photo. No, I don't think it's one of their sisters, she thought. I don't know why . . . There's something about her . . . She was wearing a long white dress and holding a tennis racquet. Her hair looked as if it had been pulled back into a loose plait. There was something about the girl's gaze that seemed familiar. It's such a piercing gaze, she thought. Who is she?

Flame looked at the photograph for some while, then placed it down on the bed beside the piles she had already made. Then she picked up another photograph – this one of two young people.

She drew the duvet round her, aware that she felt suddenly cold, but kept looking at the photographs. When Flame was absorbed, she was completely absorbed.

As she picked up the photograph of the girl again and

gave it another look, she shivered. It's so cold in here, she thought – and looked up and around the room.

And, as she did so, the hair on the back of her neck stood on end.

She heard herself breathing heavily, felt her heart pounding hard against her chest.

Oh my God, she thought.

That instant, the door burst open. Flame screamed as a fierce, icy wind blasted through her room. The enormous gust lifted the piles of photographs – *whoosh* – up to the ceiling. They spun through the air and began to spiral down to the floor.

Flame tried to get up, but she could not move. Something was holding her to the bed. Something was screaming in her ear. Something was covering her face . . .

The plan, she thought. Margaret Sprite is trying to get the plan . . .

My power, she thought. She fought and pushed and tried to breathe. Use my power . . .

The ghost breathed an icy blast into her face, so cold that she thought she would freeze. A long, thin icy hand seemed to reach out and grip her shoulder. Another hand seemed to be reaching for the plan, tucked into her shirt. She heard a woman's laugh.

'*No, no!*' she cried out, her hands covering her chest to protect the plan.

Use my power, use my power . . . power of Fire. Melt the ghost, warm up the cold air – make her go away!

With all her might, Flame Sprite summoned her power of

Fire. Her hands became hot, so hot that she thought they would frizzle and burn.

Bright red zigzags of heat surged through her arms and hands. She growled with fury. *'Go away! Leave me be!'*

As she wrestled with Margaret Sprite, she felt the ghost's power lessen.

But Margaret was quick. She made a lunge and almost reached the plan.

'NO!' cried Flame, summoning another burst of Fire. *'You will not take it!'*

Then another voice – Ash's voice – cried *'NO! Leave my sister alone!'*

In an instant, it was all over. The icy hands were gone. The scattered photographs lay still. The air warmed.

Flame collapsed on to her bed and closed her eyes.

Ash stood in the doorway, holding her hand out in mid-air. Her face was pale and she breathed hard. 'Flame? Flame – are you okay?'

She walked towards the bed, saw her elder sister's face – and burst into tears.

'Flame, wake up!' Ash said, sitting down on the bed and taking her sister's hand.

Flame opened her eyes and gave a weak smile. Her face was wet with perspiration, her hair tousled and limp. She pulled herself up on the bed and reached out to hug her sister.

For a while they sat there, together, then Flame leaned back, exhausted.

'I didn't think I could stop her,' she said, pushing her thick copper hair back from her face.

'But you did!' said Ash, with a gentle smile.

Flame reached into her shirt, to check the plan. 'Still here,' she murmured, patting it. She looked at Ash. 'What happened?'

'I was coming up to my room and my magic stone suddenly squeaked. I knew something was wrong. As I ran up the corridor, I heard you cry out. I opened your door and saw this black, swirling shape over you. I could see you wrestling with it, trying to push it away.'

'Did you see the hands?'

'Yes,' nodded Ash. 'They were horrible.' She was silent for a moment, then said, quietly, 'And I saw her face.'

'What was it like?'

'The mouth was a wide gape – and there was a lot of dark hair. The eyes were angry and glittering black.'

Flame shuddered. 'What did you do?'

'I used my power of Earth to pull her away from you and bind her to the floor,' said Ash.

'Where is she now?' asked Flame, looking around them anxiously.

'It's all right – she's gone.'

Flame pushed herself up. 'But how did Margaret get in? I used my power to protect and seal the room! How did she get past that?'

'Perhaps Glenda is using her power to make Margaret's ghost stronger.'

Flame put her face in her hands. 'Oh, that was horrible,' she said, quietly. 'Thank goodness you came up when you did.'

For a few seconds, the sisters sat silent and motionless.

'We better not say anything to Ariel, or she won't sleep,' said Flame.

'It's the plan the ghost wants – I think Ariel should be safe,' said Ash.

All over the navy carpet were scattered photographs. Ash bent down to look. Flame climbed out of bed and put the box on the floor. Together they gathered up the photographs.

'What is it you're looking for?' asked Ash.

Flame sat up, pushed her hair out of her eyes. 'There's something we need to take into the portal. I have the sense there's a photograph, somewhere.'

'What would it do?'

'Trigger some kind of memory in Margaret Sprite.'

'Oh,' said Ash, quietly.

'We have to find a way to change the past,' said Flame.

As Ash picked up the last photograph, Marina and Ariel came into the room.

'What are you doing?' asked Ariel.

Flame and Ash looked at each other, then at Ariel.

'I dropped the box and the photographs fell out,' said Flame.

Ariel looked her straight in the eye. 'No, you didn't – the ghost came, didn't it? I can feel it.'

Flame nodded. 'Yes.'

For the next half-hour, the Sprite Sisters sat on Flame's bed, as the story was told.

Ariel's face grew paler and paler. 'She might come into my room in the middle of the night,' she whispered.

Flame sat forward and grabbed her little sister's hand.

'No, listen – I don't think the ghost will bother you. It's the plan she's after – and that's here. You know what Grandma told us – about protecting ourselves when we went into our rooms?'

Ariel nodded.

'Well, we need to do it with all our power – or at least I do.'

As the sisters sat in a huddle, Mum came into the room. 'Okay, time for bed everyone,' she said. 'Busy few days ahead of us.'

When they got into their bedrooms, Marina, Ash and Ariel summoned all their power to protect their space.

As the moon rose in the late October sky, Flame lay in the dark, thinking. Her body was tired, but her mind kept ticking over.

She sat up and switched on the bedside lamp, then picked up the box of photographs.

One by one, she took out a photograph from the box, looked at it, then laid it on the duvet.

Then she came to the one of the girl with the piercing gaze.

I've seen her before, she thought. There's a photograph somewhere. Where would it be? she wondered.

It's a photograph of a group, she remembered.

There are lots of photographs in here of Sidney and his five children. I have a feeling I have seen one somewhere with six children . . .

When she came to the last photograph, Flame sat for a

second and stared at the box. It's not here, she thought. Carefully, she lifted the photographs from the duvet and placed them back in the box. Then she placed the lid on the top and lay down to sleep.

As she did so, she reached for the letter and plan, which she had placed under her pillow. She summoned all her magic power of Fire, to protect them – and her – for the night. Then she closed her eyes.

Falling, she was falling into a deep sleep – but something was jabbing in her mind.

Again, she pulled herself up on the bed.

What is it? she wondered, staring into the dark.

She yawned a huge yawn. I'm so tired, she thought. I just want to sleep – and she began to lie down again. But no, the jabbing feeling started again.

She sat up in bed and turned on the bedside light once more.

I must use my power of the East to look ahead, she thought. There is something I need to know.

For several minutes, she stared into the distance.

Then, in her mind, she saw the magic box.

The box, she thought, the photograph is in the box. Yawning, she got out of bed and went to the bookshelf at the side of the room and bent down. On the bottom shelf, she pulled out three large books and put them on the floor. Hidden behind them was the magic box – the box that George had used to hide the plan and the letter. It was small, made of wood with the shape of a crossed circle on the lid.

She took the box back to her bed and held it under the

light of the lamp. There are other things in here, thought Flame, prising open the lid.

She smiled as she saw the contents. There were the four dried rosebuds that George had picked from the garden at Sprite Towers, before he went off to the war. And there, she thought, picking up a small black and white photograph, was the photograph I'd remembered.

In the middle, sitting bolt upright, were Sidney and Mim Sprite. Around them were six children. Standing at the side, was a blond-haired girl with a piercing gaze.

Then she picked up the box that Dad had given her and rummaged through until she found the photograph of the girl and the two boys.

It's the same girl, thought Flame, comparing the images. She stared hard, her mind now beginning to whirr again. But sleep beckoned.

I don't know, she thought. I'll work it out in the morning.

She pulled out the letter and the folded-up plan from under her pillow and put them into the box, along with the two photographs. Then she pushed the box under her pillow.

It's not comfortable like this, but it's safe, she thought. I have protected it with my power.

And with that, she put her head on the pillow and fell into a deep sleep.

CHAPTER ELEVEN

THE GHOST
IN THE TOWER

THERE WAS great excitement at school on Tuesday among
the Sprite Sisters and the friends they had invited to the party.

The Sprite Sisters had spent many hours discussing who
they would invite. Flame had wanted to invite Quinn, but she
also wanted to ask her best friends, Pia and Lisha. Marina,
Ash and Ariel wanted to ask girls. In the end, Flame agreed
not to ask Quinn. He'd feel silly, she said, if he was the only
boy there. Marina had invited Su-Ling and her best friend,
Janey, Quinn's sister. Ash invited Rachel and Katie. Ariel
invited Hoshi and Fern. Since Mum had invited Verena, this
brought the total to thirteen.

Now, at break, they were all talking about the party and
their costumes.

Flame's mind was only half on the Hallowe'en party. The other half was thinking about what was happening at Sprite Towers. From time to time, she patted her blazer, to check that the plan and the letter – and the two photographs she had been studying the night before – were still inside her breast pocket.

Margaret might have got the plan last night, she thought. And she would have given it to Glenda Glass. And then what? We were lucky . . .

'You're miles away, Flame,' laughed Pia.

'Sorry,' smiled Flame. 'Lot on my mind.'

'I'm sure your costume will be stunning,' said Pia. 'We're all going to have such fun tomorrow evening. I can't wait!'

Pia's deep brown eyes shone with warmth and, for a moment, Flame's heart lightened. 'Yes,' she smiled. 'We will.'

But, when they got back from school that afternoon, Flame's heart felt heavy.

'What's the matter?' asked Marina, anxiously, as they stood in the kitchen.

'I don't know,' said Flame, shaking her head. 'I feel weird. Something's going to happen – I can feel it.'

'We'll all stay close to you, don't worry,' said Marina, touching her arm.

'It's strange without Grandma here – I miss her,' said Flame, looking round. Archie was chewing an old tennis shoe on the floor. Bert was watching him from his basket. Pudding lay curled up on the Windsor chair. On the sideboard sat the four pumpkins, their faces dark.

'Let's have a piece of cake and some tea,' said Marina,

moving to the table. 'Mum's put the kettle on.'

'Where's Mum?' asked Ariel, walking in.

'She giving a lesson,' said Marina. 'Listen, we must stay close to Flame.'

Ariel nodded. 'Okay.'

'Where's Dad?' asked Ash, coming through the door and shutting it behind her.

'He's at the office in town,' said Marina. 'Mum said to have tea.'

Marina took the kettle off the Aga hob and poured the boiling water into the teapot beside it. Then she carried it to the table.

The four Sprite Sisters sat down. Marina, Ash and Ariel exchanged worried glances, aware that Flame was quiet and distracted.

Ash cut them each a big slice of homemade fruitcake. Marina poured mugs of hot tea.

For a few minutes, they relaxed.

Flame smiled as the hot tea swilled down her throat. 'That's nice.'

'The costumes are all ready,' said Ash, through a mouthful of cake.

'It'll be such fun!' said Ariel. 'I can't wait!'

And for a few minutes, they chatted about the party. The kitchen felt warm and safe.

Archie wrestled his shoe across the floor. They watched him and laughed. 'Silly puppy!' said Ariel.

Then Flame shivered. 'Suddenly feels cold in here,' she said, looking round.

'Hm,' agreed Marina, hugging her arms around her.

'Look,' whispered Ariel, an expression of horror on her face.

'What?' said Marina, spinning round.

'Over there,' pointed Ariel, standing up.

'Oh my God!' whispered Flame, rising up in her seat. On the sideboard, the crazy faces of the pumpkins glowed menacingly.

'The ghost is here again,' said Ariel, nervously.

'The lights,' murmured Ash, looking up as the lights flickered.

'Keep close to Flame!' shouted Marina, moving towards her elder sister. Within a second, Ash was standing close by – and so was Ariel. The lights flickered again. They waited, their hearts pumping.

'Where is it?' whispered Ash. 'I can't see it, but I can feel it.'

'I don't like it!' cried Ariel, looking round.

On the floor, Archie gave a loud whine. Bert yelped in his basket.

The Sprite Sisters moved even closer together as an icy blast of air swept through the kitchen.

'Shall we use our magic power?' suggested Marina, her hands outstretched.

'Just wait,' said Flame. 'We can't use it on something we can't see – and Mum might come in.'

They waited, breathing hard and their hearts pounding.

Then – quite suddenly – the air cleared and was warm again.

Ash turned towards the sideboard and exclaimed, 'Look – the pumpkins have gone out!'

'It's gone,' said Flame, looking round the kitchen.

'Thank goodness,' said Marina, flopping down into a chair at the table.

Flame, Ash and Ariel sat in their chairs and, for a few seconds, they were silent.

Suddenly, Ash's stone emitted a loud *beep*. She started in surprise. 'What now?' she exclaimed, pulling it out of her pocket and looking at it. 'Something's happened,' she said, standing up.

Flame, Marina and Ariel jumped up and looked around the room.

'I can't see anything,' murmured Flame.

'There's something wrong,' said Ash.

Ariel was bending down, looking under the table and around the floor. 'Bert's in his basket – but where's Archie?' she said, her voice rising. 'Can anyone see Archie?'

In an instant, Flame, Marina and Ash were on the floor.

'*He's gone!*' squeaked Ariel. '*She's taken him!*'

'Sssh!' said Marina. 'Be quiet – Mum will hear!'

Flame stood up, and clenched her fists. '*The tower!*' she said. 'She'll have taken him to the tower!'

'*Quick!*' said Ash, her face ashen-white.

In the dining room, Mum heard the din as her daughters pounded up the staircase. Her piano pupil – a serious-looking young man – was halfway through his exam piece. Mum looked round at the door. Whatever's going on? she wondered.

'Excuse me a moment,' she said, and she got up and opened the door. She walked through to the hallway, looked up, saw – and heard – the girls running up to the attics. What are they doing? she wondered. She turned, and saw her pupil's anxious face watching her through the open door.

'I'm so sorry,' she said, coming back and sitting down. 'Pick up from where you were.'

At the top of the stairs, Flame stopped. 'Which tower?' she shouted, looking from left to right along the attics corridor.

'That one!' said Marina, seeing the door of the West Tower swinging open. She hurtled along the corridor, her sisters close behind.

At the door, Flame caught her breath. 'Wait! We must use our magic power to protect ourselves before we go up there!'

For a few seconds they stood there, each focusing their minds to create invisible shields around them.

Then Flame said, 'Ready?'

Ash and Ariel nodded.

'Hang on, Flame,' said Marina, clutching her arm. 'You know why Margaret's drawn you up here, don't you?'

Flame felt into her shirt. 'The plan's here – I've got it.'

'Whatever happens, just keep hold of it,' said Marina. 'I'll go first. Ash, you go behind Flame.'

Ash flicked the light switch at the side of the door, as Marina charged up the rickety steps. Flame went next. Ash, then Ariel, followed close behind.

'He's here!' cried Marina, reaching the top. 'Archie's here!'

'Careful!' shouted Flame, stepping up behind her. In a second, the four Sprite Sisters were standing in the wide, round room. High above them was the dome of glass.

'Stay close to Flame!' cried Ash, as Marina dived to pick up the little puppy. Quickly, she grabbed Archie and moved back to stand by her sisters.

'Make a circle around Flame!' shouted Ash.

'The air is like ice!' said Ariel.

'She's here!' said Flame, quietly. 'I can feel her.'

Marina, Ash and Ariel stood, looking out, their backs to their tall, elder sister. In the middle, Flame moved in a slow circle, gazing at the dome. Her fingers tingled as she felt her magic power of Fire building up.

A harsh, cackling laugh burst out above their heads. The girls jumped in surprise and looked up.

'Where *is* she?' hissed Marina, through gritted teeth.

'I'm scared!' whispered Ariel.

'Stay calm, Ariel,' said Ash.

'Keep close!' shouted Marina, her left arm tightly around Archie, her right hand poised to use her power.

Suddenly, over their heads, a swirling black shape appeared. It dived and spun, up and down, round and round. Long thin hands stretched out of the shape, reaching at their heads.

Ariel screamed.

Then up it went again. The four girls craned their heads, their eyes focused on the swirling shape, their fingers poised and ready to use their magic.

'What's she going to do?' squeaked Ariel.

'I don't know, pumpkin,' said Flame. Her heart pumped so hard she thought it would burst through her shirt. She could feel the incredible strength of Margaret's dark power.

The black, whirling form hovered right over the top of them. Flame's hands were tight with tension as she pointed her fingers.

Marina, Ash and Ariel moved closer around her. Then,

'*Quickly – all together!*' Flame shouted, as the ghost dived straight down at her.

Flame ducked, bending her body across the plan, as Marina, Ash and Ariel used their magic. With a great crackle of blue light, their powers of Water, Earth and Air whooshed out of their fingers straight towards the ghost of Margaret Sprite. Their powers merged into a ball of blue light around the swirling black shape. Ariel used her power to spin and lift the ball of light. Round and round it went, right up to the big glass dome. All the time, the ball seemed to be getting smaller, as Ash used her binding power to shrink the ghost's power.

Marina, Ash and Ariel brought down their hands and waited.

'It's going,' murmured Ariel, with a sigh of relief.

For a few seconds, all was still. The girls moved in a slow circle, still looking up.

'No, it's not!' said Flame. 'It's coming back!'

As she said this, the ghost swelled in size and dived towards Flame Sprite. 'Ha, ha, ha, ha, ha . . .' went the cackling laugh.

Flame was furious. She stood tall and raised her right hand. 'How dare you try to hurt us!' she shouted, pointing her fingers at the ghost.

As it hurtled towards them, Flame used every bit of her magic power of Fire.

A huge crack – like a bolt of lightning – whooshed out of her fingers and hit the swirling black form. There was a hideous scream, a spark of bright light – and then it was gone.

In the middle of the tower room, the Sprite Sisters waited, their hearts pounding hard. Each of them looked around, watchful, silent. After a minute, Marina said, 'I think it's gone.'

'For the moment,' murmured Flame, looking down at her hand. 'Blimey, that was strong power.'

'How did you make it?' asked Marina, her arm still around Archie.

Flame shook her head. 'I felt so angry – and my power seemed to get very strong.'

'Well, be careful, sis – you know what happened to Grandma when she felt angry and used her power against Glenda,' said Marina.

Flame glanced at her and nodded.

'Are you okay?' Marina asked Flame.

Her elder sister nodded. 'My fingers are still tingling, but I think they're okay.'

'Will the ghost come back?' whispered Ariel.

'I expect so,' said Flame, looking up at the glass dome. 'I think we're safe for now, but we must go into the portal as soon as possible.'

With a sense of relief, the four girls came together and clutched each other tight. Archie licked their hands as they stroked him.

'Come on, let's go down,' said Marina.

'We must get Archie back to the kitchen,' said Ash. 'Mum will have a fit if she thinks we've taken him upstairs.'

The four sisters looked up once more at the glass dome. All was still.

They clambered down the rickety wooden stairs, closed the tower room door and crept along the attics corridor. At the top of the staircase, they looked over the banister rail to the hallway.

Down below, they heard their mother call, 'Goodnight,' as she closed the front door.

Then the telephone rang. Mum picked it up. 'Charles, hello! We thought you'd ring this evening. Are you coming to see us this weekend?'

The Sprite Sisters watched as she walked back into the dining room, holding the telephone, then made their way downstairs as quickly and as quietly as possible.

'She's talking to Charles Smythson,' whispered Ash.

'I wish he wasn't coming here again,' groaned Flame. 'We have enough to worry about.'

In the dining room, Mum chatted and laughed. The four girls passed by the open door in a huddle. Just as they got into the kitchen and put Archie in his basket, Dad came through the front door. He strode across the hallway, poked his head into the dining room and waved at Mum, then marched into the kitchen.

'Evening, girls!' he said, smiling and, dumping his leather briefcase on the table. 'What have you all been up to then?'

Flame gave a wry smile. 'You'd never believe us if we told you!'

'Try me!' he countered, but was distracted by Ash, who came up to kiss him.

'Did you have a nice day, Daddy?' she asked.

'Yes, thanks, love,' he said, bending down to kiss her. He ruffled her tufty chestnut hair affectionately, then looked round. 'Sounds as if Charles will be up this weekend.'

'How long's he staying?' asked Flame.

'No idea – I expect Mum will tell us in a minute. Right, let's get some supper started, shall we?'

CHAPTER TWELVE

FLAME'S 'FEELING'

LATER THAT evening, when Mum had gone downstairs, Marina, Ash and Ariel gathered on Flame's bed.

'Do you think we should have told Mum and Dad about the ghost kidnapping Archie?' said Ash, her chin on her hand.

'No, they've got enough to think about,' said Flame. 'And, besides – there's nothing they can do.'

'Why didn't the ghost just make Archie disappear, like the hat?' asked Ariel.

'Maybe it's easier to make an object disappear than a living thing,' suggested Ash.

'Hm,' said Marina, thoughtfully. 'Or maybe she wanted us to find him.'

'I hope he's safe down there now,' said Ash.

'What shall we do about the party tomorrow?' asked Ariel.

'What do you mean?' asked Flame.

'So far, Margaret has terrified the living daylights out of us four,' said Ariel. 'She may want to scare all our friends to bits as well.'

Marina looked thoughtful. 'Ariel's right – and what would we do?'

They were silent for a moment.

Flame looked down at the red duvet, chewed her lip. 'If Margaret appears – and she may well do so – I think we should act as if the ghost is part of the party, as if we expected it.'

'But Margaret could do anything!' exclaimed Ariel. 'She's bonkers! It was bad enough fighting Glenda – but this – this – is *horrible*!'

'But we can't cancel the party now,' said Ash. 'What would we say to Mum and Dad?'

This thought hung in the air.

'And after the party, we go into the portal,' said Marina.

'Yes – but only after we have found this object that George talked about,' added Flame.

'And fully understand Margaret, he said,' added Marina.

'Yes, that as well,' agreed Flame.

Ariel rested her chin on her hands and gave a low moan. 'I don't want to go into the portal again!'

Flame put her arm around her sister's shoulder. 'We have to do this together, Ariel. I know you're young – but we need you. We must stick together.'

Ariel looked up at her. 'Yes,' she said, quietly.

Flame's eyes were bright and sharp. 'You know that

expression, "The whole is greater than the sum of the parts"? Have you heard that?'

Ariel nodded.

'Well, it's the same with us,' said Flame. 'We're each powerful in our own right, but if we work together and balance our magic, we are much, much more powerful. That's why Glenda hasn't been able to beat us. She's used some very dark magic against us, but we've always been able to hold her back. We have to believe that we can do this with Margaret.'

'But what are we going to do?' asked Ariel.

'We will be going back in time. We will see Margaret as she used to be. She won't be a ghost – she will be real, like George was the other day. Margaret will be standing there *in front of us*.'

Her sisters' faces were thoughtful.

Then Flame reached into the pocket of her pyjama top, pulled out the two photographs and handed them to her sisters. 'I've felt very drawn to these two old family photographs,' she said.

Marina and Ash studied the group photograph of Sidney and Mim and the six children.

Ariel stared at the photograph of young Frederick and George standing with the girl with the piercing eyes.

'Who's that girl?' asked Flame. 'I know that gaze!'

'Mrs Duggery,' replied Ariel in a matter-of-fact voice.

'Mrs Duggery?' said Flame, amazed. 'Give it here.'

Flame stared at the photograph again. She thought of the strange old lady who had appeared in their lives that summer, with her lilac knitted hat and big brown boots. Mrs Duggery had the most powerful magic of all the Sprites. She had helped the girls save Sprite Towers when Glenda Glass and Oswald Foffington-Plinker tried to get the old house from the Sprites. 'Yes, I think you're right . . .' Flame's voice trailed off.

'Show us,' said Marina, holding out her hand.

They swapped photographs. Marina and Ash looked hard at the blond-haired girl. 'I think you're right, Ariel,' said Ash.

'But that would make Mrs Duggery about a hundred and ten years old!' exclaimed Marina.

Flame laughed. 'Why are we surprised?'

The four sisters giggled. 'Do you remember how she marched across the top of the roof, holding huge piles of pantiles?' said Ash.

'And Dad saw her up there and didn't believe his eyes!' laughed Marina.

'He couldn't believe she could carry a wardrobe on her own – and she's so tiny!' added Ariel.

'She's scary,' smiled Ash.

'Super-human,' agreed Marina. She looked again at the photograph. 'Mrs Duggery! Of course! It's the piercing gaze.'

'She was very pretty,' said Ariel.

'Yes,' agreed Marina. 'But she wasn't wearing a lilac knitted hat and huge brown boots then!'

Ariel giggled.

'I don't understand, Flame,' said Ash, turning to her sister. 'What's the connection between Mrs Duggery and Margaret and the portal?'

Flame shook her head. 'I don't know yet, but I must work it out quickly. We can't go into the portal until we are fully protected.'

'But how will you know if we are or not?' exclaimed Ash. 'We haven't done it before! How could you know?'

Flame's green eyes looked troubled. 'We must act soon.'

The four sisters sighed heavily.

Marina and Ariel handed the photographs to Flame. She put them back in her pyjama pocket, then said, 'I keep getting the word "remember" in my mind . . .'

'Is it something Margaret has to remember?' asked Marina. 'Something she has forgotten?'

'Yes,' nodded Flame.

'Let's all think about it,' said Marina, looking round at the clock on Flame's bedside table. 'Come on, it's late. We'd better go to sleep now. We're going to be up late tomorrow.'

'I don't want to go into my bedroom alone,' said Ariel. 'The ghost could be anywhere.'

At this thought, the sisters all looked worried. Then Marina said, 'I'll come with you, Ariel. Then you must seal your room – like Grandma told you. We all must.'

A minute later, when Marina, Ash and Ariel had gone back to their bedrooms, Flame lifted the box of photographs on to her bed once more. One by one, she sifted through the images. All those lives, she thought. All those stories . . .

Nothing. She could not find it, this thing she was looking for. One by one, the photographs came out, on to the duvet. Soon the box was empty. Flame sighed heavily. Oh well, she thought, I'll have another look tomorrow. I *must* find it before we go into the portal . . .

* * *

As the Sprite Sisters settled to sleep, Glenda Glass stared out of the window at the garden of The Oaks, one mile away.

In her mind, she talked to her grandmother's ghost – could see her moving restlessly around the attics at Sprite Towers.

Margaret had succeeded in scaring the girls in the tower that evening – that she could see in her mind – but she still hadn't got hold of the secret plan. Flame Sprite is protecting it well, Glenda thought.

The girls' powers are getting stronger, she thought. I can feel it. They have more protection around them. Perhaps Marilyn has helped them – or Mrs Duggery. That woman was always getting in the way, she thought, with a grim smile.

Glenda called to Margaret in her head. 'Grandmother, get me that plan. We will have Sprite Towers, you and I. You will have your house back! You will have your revenge!'

She saw Margaret moving down the attic stairs and along the second-floor corridor. 'That's right, Grandmother! Scare the little one!'

The swirling ball of energy stopped at Ariel's door.

'Go in!' said Glenda. 'Go through!'

But the ghost could not pass. Ariel's magic had sealed the door and the youngest Sprite Sister slept quietly.

Glenda Glass groaned with frustration, then she called once more to her grandmother in her mind: 'It's the Hallowe'en party tomorrow, Margaret. You can give the Sprite family something to think about then. We will get what we want, Grandmother. We will get it all.'

CHAPTER THIRTEEN

THE HALLOWE'EN PARTY

By HALF past six on Wednesday evening, everything was ready for the party. Log fires blazed in the library and the drawing room. The kitchen was aglow with candles and the four eerie pumpkins. In the middle of the room was the table, spread with the Hallowe'en feast. As the Sprite family gathered, there was much shrieking and laughter.

'You look hideous!' exclaimed Ash to her parents. Mum and Dad stood, stiff as boards, their arms held out straight, their heads tipped to one side.

'We're zombie doctors!' said Dad, rolling his 'dead' eyes. His face was chalky white and his eyes had huge red rims. His gelled chestnut-brown hair stood up like a thatch and he wore a white doctor's coat. Around his neck hung a stethoscope, covered in 'blood'.

Beside him, Mum moved in a jerky manner. Her wavy blond hair was back-combed into a huge, frizzy mess and her chalky face broken by a mouth that was a jagged slash of dark red. Large pools of 'blood' covered her white doctor's coat.

Mum burst out laughing. 'Look at you all!' she exclaimed, seeing her daughters. There was Flame, the mystic witch, in her silky red dress and long red gloves. A deep green scarf was tied over her head; underneath this, her copper-coloured hair spread wide. The skin on her face was pale green and her lips were two lines of black. Her eyelids were painted a deep emerald, and along the top of her lashes she had drawn sweeping black lines.

Marina drew back the hood of her black velvet cloak and hissed at them, snapping her vampire's teeth and tearing the air with her long white nails. Her face was deathly white and 'blood' dripped down her chin. Ash – a sleek black cat complete with whiskers – snarled and clawed, while Ariel leaped about as a skeleton.

Then the doorbell rang. 'Off we go!' said Dad.

And in they came: Flame's friends, Pia and Lisha, were dressed as a spider witch and a gothic princess. Marina's friends, Janey and Su-Ling, were a red devil and a midnight fairy. Ash's friend, Katie, was a corpse bride, while Rachel was a vampire. Hoshi, Ariel's friend, made a lot of noise as a howling ghoul, while Fern flapped about as a bat.

Last to arrive was Verena Glass, who glided in, looking absolutely amazing, dressed as a rainbow sorceress.

Suddenly, the kitchen of Sprite Towers was full of giggling

and shrieking 'creatures'. Standing in the candlelight, they held fizzy drinks and admired each other's costumes.

In the relaxed, warm atmosphere, the Sprite Sisters and their parents tried to put the ghost to the back of their minds. 'It'll be fine – don't worry,' Dad reassured Mum, several times. The Sprite Sisters were less optimistic. For them, it was a question of 'when' Margaret appeared, rather then 'if'. But they were soon caught up in the excitement and fun.

Much fuss was made of Archie. Bert looked on with disdain as the girls drooled over the little black puppy.

'He's *soooo* sweet!' twittered Fern, stroking his tummy.

Then it was time to eat. Each armed with a plate, they tucked into the spread of delicious food. In the middle of the table, Flame's toffee apples stood straight like soldiers.

'These are wicked!' said Lisha, grabbing a baked prune wrapped round with bacon.

'They're called "Devils on Horseback"!' laughed Flame.

'This is so cool!' giggled Katie, slurping a lurid mint-green milkshake.

'I hope we're going to play Sardines – it'd be amazing with all the cupboards here,' said Janey.

Marina nodded, her mouth full of burger and bun. 'Yes,' she replied, as she swallowed. 'That's what we're planning.'

'Let's put out all the lights – then it will be really spooky!' said Verena.

Mum walked round, offering the girls plates of food, while Dad filled up their fizzy drinks.

From time to time, each of the Sprite Sisters looked around at the pumpkins – but they looked normal. There were no 'eyes' this evening, and the girls relaxed into the party.

After the feast, they all went through to the drawing room, the biggest room in the house. Dad was the umpire as the girls divided into two teams to play Pass the Apple. Mum joined in to even up the numbers. There was much laughter as the two teams each tried to pass their apple from chin to chin, without anyone using their hands. Then they did Wrap the Mummy with a lot of loo roll, and some code-busting with Dad's special Hallowe'en Secret Message Puzzle.

After a quick drink, it was time to play Sardines. Mum held out a hat holding thirteen pieces of folded paper and they all dived in. Ash's friend, Rachel, was the first Sardine. The tall, dark-haired vampire left the room and shut the door behind her. Quickly, she walked through to the pantry at the side of the kitchen and pulled the door to behind her. It was dark and cold in there, but she waited, excited and alert.

Half a minute later, the other twelve girls ran through the huge house. They spread out, opening doors, searching behind pieces of furniture, looking in cupboards. Most went upstairs, three looked downstairs. Each time Rachel was 'found', the 'finder' hid with her in the pantry. Every so often another girl joined the growing group of 'sardines'. The last girl still looking was little Hoshi: Mum alerted her to the chattering in the pantry.

'Found you!' she shouted, yanking open the door. Everyone was smiling. 'That was great!' they laughed, as they came out of the pantry. 'Can we do another Sardines?'

Flame whispered to Marina. 'So far, so good.'

'Let's hope it stays that way,' whispered Marina.

'It's a great party,' Ash said quietly, coming up beside them. 'Everyone's really enjoying it.'

Then it was back to the drawing room, where Mum held out the hat again.

Everyone was fizzing with excitement as Pia drew out the 'Sardine'. She knew the house well and ran up the stairs to the attics. There, she turned right and walked along the corridor to a big cupboard by the West Tower. She opened the door, walked in, pulled the door to – and waited, her pulse quickening.

A minute later, the girls charged through the house searching for Pia. Again, they spread out, each working alone. The witch and the vampires, the ghoul, bat, black cat, corpse bride, midnight fairy, red devil and the sorceress moved silently through the house, looking, looking.

Flame was about to mount the stairs when the lights flickered – and went out. For a moment, the house was plunged into darkness. Flame gasped. Oh no – please not this evening, she thought.

As the lights flickered on again, she spun round and looked up the staircase. An icy draft whooshed past her. Suddenly, it was not finding Pia that concerned her: it was finding the ghost. She patted her dress to check the plan was still safely stuffed down the front, lifted her red silk skirt and ran up the stairs to the first-floor corridor.

Down in the kitchen, Mum and Dad, the 'zombies', were clearing up the feast as the lights went out. 'Oh no, not tonight,' said Mum, anxiously. As the lights sputtered on again, they exchanged worried glances.

'I'm sure it will all be okay, love,' said Dad, looking around.

Upstairs, Flame opened the doors on the first floor. Various girls were creeping about, but everyone tried to avoid each other.

The ghost isn't here, she thought, looking round. I'd feel it . . .

Quickly, she ran up to the second floor and walked into her bedroom, then each of her sisters' rooms. As she came out of Ash's room, the lights flickered again. She stood still, waited. The lights in the house seemed to be dimmer than usual. It's dark, thought Flame. What's going on?

Something brushed past her face. Suddenly, all her senses were alive. It was as if she could hear every sound, sense every movement in the air. The ghost is close, she thought, her body tensing. Then – someone's coming . . .

She drew back slightly, moved into the corner beside Ash's door.

Hidden in the shadow, Flame watched as Verena crept past and opened the door to Marina's room – and walked in, looking for the Sardines. A few seconds later, she came out and looked around, up and down the corridor. Flame held her breath. Verena was standing about five metres away – but she hadn't seen her.

The air felt icy cold.

It's here, thought Flame, her breathing quickening, her heart beginning to race.

She's felt it too, thought Flame, as she saw the tall, blond-haired girl turn slowly, as if she was following something.

And there it was – the ghost of Margaret Sprite was circling Verena Glass!

Flame watched, amazed, intrigued. This time the ghost was not whirling with menace.

There's something – something almost friendly about the way the ghost is moving around Verena, she thought. It's almost like a dance . . .

It's weird, thought Flame, her eyes narrowing. Does the ghost know that this girl is her great-great-granddaughter? Perhaps Glenda has told her . . .

Does Verena sense something? What is she feeling? Why is she smiling like that? She's not frightened, thought Flame. She's just *watching* the ghost . . .

A shiver of cold passed through Flame so suddenly that she coughed. *Blast*, she thought, covering her mouth. She looked up. Verena was staring into the shadow. Their eyes met. She's looking at me, thought Flame. She knows I have seen the ghost moving around her . . .

Verena turned, quickly, and walked back up the corridor. Flame waited for a moment, heard Verena's tread on the stairs going up to the attics. Where's the ghost gone, thought Flame. Where is it now?

In the big cupboard by the West Tower, Pia had waited patiently. It was about five minutes before Lisha found her. Together, they whispered in the dark, until the door was opened – and in came Katie. 'Sardine!' she giggled.

'Quickly, come in – someone will see you!' said Pia, pulling her in. Within another few minutes, Janey opened the door, saw the corridor light catch their faces, laughed, and crept in. And then Ash found them, too. 'Meoww,' she whispered. 'Can I come in?'

The five girls talked softly, all the time wondering who would be the next person to open the door of the cupboard. Ash was standing by the door.

The handle turned and the door began to open.

Ash started – she knew immediately that it was not a girl opening the door.

It's the ghost, she gasped, her body tensing with fear. *What do I do?* I can't use my magic power here! Margaret Sprite's outside – and there are girls in here!

As the door opened, a whoosh of freezing cold rushed through the cupboard, touching the girls' faces.

The five girls gasped and stared at the door. A thin white hand reached in – just visible in the dim light. Pia and Katie shrieked. Janey screamed. '*What is it?*' cried Lisha.

The girls froze in horror as the door opened a little further. A black wraithlike shape moved into the cupboard – and hung over their heads. Two long white hands protruded from the shape, as if it was about to grasp one of them.

'It's a ghost!' cried Pia. 'It's a ghost!'

Lisha screamed loudly. Janey screamed louder. Katie burst into tears, hid her face in her hands – and began to slump to the floor.

'Katie's fainted!' cried Lisha, taking the girl's weight.

Ash grabbed Katie's other arm. Suddenly there was chaos. Everyone tried to get out of the cupboard at once.

At the same time, the whirling black form above them

spun faster and faster, until it seemed to shrink into a ball. Then, in an instant, it sped off along the corridor, passing Verena Glass, who stood outside the door.

As Ash came out of the cupboard, trying to hold up Katie, she turned – saw the ghost disappear. She realised that Verena was standing there and caught her eye.

She's seen it, thought Ash. Then she shouted to the girls in the cupboard, 'It's okay! Look – there's nothing there!'

But the girls scrambling to get out were not listening. They'd seen a ghost! Everybody was shouting.

Through the big house, everyone else heard the commotion and rushed up to the attics. As the girls scrambled on to the corridor, Verena Glass stood a few metres away, watching them. Her eyes met Ash's. Ash turned away, struggling to keep Katie upright as Lisha seemed to have let go of her.

'Did you see it? Did you see it, Verena?' Janey cried, waving her arms about.

'It was a ghost!' shouted Pia. 'I *saw* it!'

'That was *so* spooky!' exclaimed Lisha, her eyes wide as saucers.

Marina dashed up, saw Ash and immediately went to help her.

'Did you see it?' Janey asked Verena again.

Verena stood, cool as a cucumber, and shook her head. 'No, I didn't see anything,' she said. As Flame came up behind her, she turned. The two girls held each other's gaze for a second. Then Verena smiled the faintest of smiles: a smile that said, 'I saw it – and I *know*'. Flame nodded the tiniest nod, as if to say, 'Yes, I know you know.'

Thank goodness she hasn't said anything, thought Flame. She quickly walked up to Ash and whispered, 'Where's the ghost gone?'

'Along the corridor – God knows where it is now!' whispered Ash, through gritted teeth.

Then, in a flash, everybody was upstairs. Hoshi, Fern and Rachel were all shouting, 'What's happened?' Dad was marching along the corridor, shouting, 'What's going on?' Coming up behind him, Mum was white-faced.

'We saw a ghost!' said Lisha to Dad. 'It came into the cupboard! It was *horrible*!'

'Really?' said Dad, rubbing his chin. 'This *is* a Hallowe'en party – and you never know what you'll come across at Sprite Towers.'

Meanwhile, Mum grabbed Katie's arm from Ash. 'It's okay, Katie,' said Mum. 'Colin – can you help here, please!'

Dad moved swiftly and grabbed Katie's other arm. Together, they sat the ashen-faced girl on a chair and pushed her head down between her knees.

'Just stay like that for a minute, Katie,' said Mum.

Around them, in the corridor, some of the girls were chattering loudly. Mum turned and said in a loud, authoritative voice. 'Now *calm down*, everyone. You've all got too excited.'

Katie sat up and tried to find her feet.

'Let's take her down, Colin,' said Mum, briskly, and they took Katie gently under the arms.

'Right, everyone, let's go downstairs to the kitchen,' Mum announced.

'Yes, come on,' said Dad, firmly.

Flame checked there was no one left in the cupboard and shut the door, then brought up the rear, as they all made their way down the wide mahogany staircase.

The faces of the Sprite Sisters were tight and drawn.

'We'll never hear the end of this,' whispered Marina, coming up beside Ash and Ariel.

'What do we say?' whispered Ariel.

'Don't tell them anything, Ariel – promise me!' implored Ash, quietly. 'Just say you don't know.'

Ariel nodded.

'Has it gone now, Flame?' whispered Marina.

Flame nodded. 'I think so.'

'Have you still got the plan?' whispered Ash.

Flame nodded, and patted the front of her dress.

All the way down the staircase, the chattering continued.

Lisha kept asking, 'Did you see it?'

'It was just a trick of the light,' said Marina.

'But what was that freezing cold air then?' said Janey. 'You must have felt that!'

'It's always cold in the attics,' replied Marina.

'And the hands – where did they come from?' asked Lisha. 'I saw hands!'

'Why did Katie faint?' asked Fern, waving her bat wings.

Ten minutes later, they were all sitting in the kitchen, cups of hot chocolate in hand. Flame's sticky ginger cake was passed round – and everyone began to relax. Katie quickly revived as she munched the cake.

'I'm so sorry, Mrs Sprite,' she smiled, shyly.

'No need to be sorry!' said Mum, kindly. 'I'm sorry you were frightened.'

When Lisha started up again, Mum said, quietly but firmly, 'Lisha, *please*. That's enough now.'

Lisha looked hurt. 'But what *was* it that we saw, Mrs Sprite?'

There was a tense silence. Everyone looked at Mum. She drew a sharp breath and looked around at the girls. She caught Dad's glance and looked at him as if to say, 'What should we tell them?'

The Sprite Sisters exchanged worried glances. Then Mum looked at Lisha and smiled. 'In answer to your question, I don't know what it was you saw. But I'm very sorry that this has happened and that you've been upset.'

'Could it have been a ghost?' asked Lisha, quietly.

Mum nodded, unable to lie. 'Yes, it's possible.'

'Has there ever been a ghost at Sprite Towers before?' asked Hoshi, standing beside Mum.

Mum smiled. 'Not as far as we know, Hoshi.'

For a few seconds, everyone was silent. Then Rachel burst out, 'Well, *I* don't care if it was a ghost or not – I think it was the best game of Sardines I've ever played!'

'So do I!' echoed Hoshi.

'And it's the best Hallowe'en party I've ever been to!' said Lisha, with a huge smile.

'Well, that's good!' laughed Mum.

The Sprite Sisters looked at one another. 'Thank heavens,' they seemed to say.

Then Dad asked Mum, 'Some music?'

'Good idea,' she said.

Everyone mucked in. The tension quickly dispelled as the table was lifted to the side of the kitchen and the chairs moved out the way. Archie was passed from girl to girl. Flame put on some loud music and immediately the girls began to dance.

'Let's go through,' Dad said to Mum.

'Good idea,' she replied.

Bert followed them to the drawing room, while Pudding dived out of the door to the peace and quiet of the garden.

And, for the next half-hour, until it was time to go home, Mum and Dad – the two zombie doctors – flopped on the sofa, exhausted, as the thirteen girls boogied around the kitchen.

At half past nine, the driveway was full of parents and cars. There was lots of laughter as the girls came out of the front door. Each of them thanked Colin and Ottalie Sprite warmly and told them it was the best Hallowe'en they'd ever had – even Katie.

'See you tomorrow!' the Sprite Sisters shouted to their friends.

Glenda Glass was the last to arrive and was about to get out of the car, when Verena saw her and walked over.

A moment later, they were driving along the narrow country lane to The Oaks. Verena's face was flushed with excitement.

'You look as if you've had fun,' said Glenda, glancing at her granddaughter.

'It was a great party,' said Verena, smiling.

'Looks as if there were some wonderful costumes.'

'Yes – they were amazing! Mr and Mrs Sprite were zombie doctors – they were so funny!'

Verena was silent for a moment, then she giggled. 'You'll never guess what happened!'

Glenda smiled to herself. I already know, she thought.

'I saw the ghost!' exclaimed Verena, her face flushed. 'It was incredible!'

'Oh,' said Glenda. 'And what did it do?'

'It was weird,' said Verena. 'I was walking along the second-floor corridor and it came up to me. It sort of whirled around me.' And she described circles in the air around her head, with her hands.

'Were you frightened?'

'No, it didn't feel unfriendly,' said Verena. 'It seemed to like me.' She was silent for a moment, then went on, 'Why would I think that? How would I know if a ghost likes me or not? I've never seen a ghost before!'

Glenda smiled mysteriously. 'Perhaps you have more abilities than you realise.'

'What do you mean?' Verena turned, looking at her grand-mother's handsome, sharp profile.

But Glenda was silent as she turned the car into the drive-way of The Oaks and stopped outside the front door.

Verena waited. Glenda stayed in her seat, then turned to Verena. 'The ghost you saw was the spirit of Margaret Sprite – your great-great-grandmother.'

'How do you know?'

'When the engineers drilled the well at Sprite Towers, they released Margaret Sprite's ghost,' said Glenda, her long, thin hand still holding the steering wheel. She stared into the dark, a thoughtful look on her face.

'But how do you *know*?' repeated Verena.

Glenda turned, and smiled at her granddaughter. 'I have certain abilities, Verena.'

Verena waited for an explanation, but Glenda offered none. They were silent for a few seconds, then Verena said, with a pensive face, 'There was something else . . .'

Glenda caught her glance.

'Flame Sprite. She was watching me with the ghost. She was hidden in the shadow in the corner and I didn't see her at first. But then she coughed – and I saw her. I could see by the look on her face that she'd seen the ghost, too.'

'Did you say anything to her?'

Verena shook her head. 'No, I just looked at her. She knew I'd seen her – and that I knew she'd seen the ghost whirling round me. It was as if we both understood something – something secret. I didn't tell any of the girls at the party that I'd seen the ghost, although they asked me.'

They got out of the car and went into the house. In the kitchen, Glenda boiled the kettle and Verena sat down. Her face was still bubbling with enjoyment.

'Then what happened?' asked Glenda, getting out the teapot.

'Well – then – gosh – it all went mad!' laughed Verena, and she described the commotion that had ensued and how Katie had fainted. 'The girls in the cupboard were terrified! They said they felt this freezing cold air – and saw these long, thin hands stretch out to grab them! Then Mr and Mrs Sprite dashed upstairs and grabbed Katie. They told everyone to come downstairs and calm down. So we went into the kitchen and we danced for the last bit. That was cool.'

'And was the grandmother there, at the party?'

'No – they said she was still in France.'

A minute later, Glenda poured the tea and sat down. As they sipped their tea, she looked at her granddaughter. How beautiful Verena is, she thought. She's so like me, when I was young . . .

Verena smiled, still giggling inside. 'It was a wonderful party! I wish I could have a party like that!' Then her face clouded. 'Hm . . .' she said, quietly.

'Tell me about the ghost,' said Glenda, leaning forward. 'Did you see a face?'

Verena pursed her lips, stared at the floor. 'It was weird. I couldn't see any face – but I *could*.'

'How do you mean?'

'Well, it was this sort of whirling, swirling black shape with long, white hands.' Verena looked at her grandmother. 'What was weird was that, somewhere in my mind, I knew the face of this "thing".'

'Margaret, your great-great-grandmother, you mean,' reminded Glenda.

'Yes, Margaret. Well, somewhere in me, I could "see" her face, as she would have been when she was human. Does that make sense?'

Glenda nodded. 'You were connecting with a memory.'

'But I've never seen a photograph of Margaret, so how would I know what she looked like?'

'Memories can be held in the minds of a family, long after something has happened,' said Glenda. 'They are passed on in our unconscious minds and can be held for generations. You may not think you know something, but, in some deep part of your mind, you *do*.'

Verena gazed at her grandmother, confused by this idea. Then Glenda said, 'What did Margaret look like, when you "saw" her in your mind?'

'She had thick, dark hair and dark, glinting eyes – and a strong face. And I seemed to hear her *say* something at the same time . . .'

Glenda waited, alert.

Verena snorted. 'I'm sure I heard her say, "magic power"!'

Glenda gave a quick smile.

'Does that mean anything to you, Grandma?'

'Yes.'

'What? Please tell me.'

Glenda looked at her granddaughter. 'You will find out, when the time comes, Verena. Now it's time for bed. We'll talk about this again, another time.'

Verena sighed – she knew there was no arguing with her grandmother. She stood up and took her mug to the sink.

Glenda waited, then said, 'I want you to watch the Sprites, Verena. And, as before, I want you to tell me everything you hear about what's happening at Sprite Towers. It's important.'

Verena sighed. 'Night, Grandma.'

Without kissing her grandmother goodnight, she walked up to her huge bedroom, with its lush designer fabrics and its stylish bathroom. Usually, she felt lonely up there, but tonight, she felt happy.

I really like the Sprites, she thought, as she drew the curtains.

A few minutes later, she lay in bed staring up into the dark, her arms crossed behind her head. I share something with Flame, she thought. We both know something the other knows. She saw I was not frightened like the other girls, and I know that she kept quiet about it.

Her mind began to whirr. There were so many questions. What was the ghost telling me? What did Grandma mean about 'when the time comes'? What is this time? What does 'magic power' mean? Why did Flame not say anything to me, when she saw me with the ghost?

Then her thoughts turned to her parents. I have so much to tell Daddy, when I see him at the weekend. I wonder if he's spoken to Mummy yet about her coming back . . .

And with that, she fell into a deep sleep.

Downstairs, in the drawing room, Glenda sat on the plush cream sofa. A cold smile crept across her face as a new thought crossed her mind.

If Verena could see the ghost, does she, too, share the Sprite family magic power? And if so, is her power awakening?

Glenda gazed across the room. We have done well, Margaret, she thought. Thank you for your help. We haven't got the secret plan yet, but I have learned something important, something that will help us further.

CHAPTER FOURTEEN

AFTER THE PARTY

THE KITCHEN of Sprite Towers felt warm and friendly on Thursday morning as the family ate breakfast. Dad had removed the pumpkins the night before while he and Mum were clearing up. This morning, there were no ghosts and icy drafts, just the heat of the Aga.

'What a party!' said Ariel, as they tucked into scrambled eggs and toast.

'Fantastic!' agreed Marina, through a mouthful of food.

'Yes – wonderful,' said Mum, smiling. 'Though we could've done without the ghost scaring everyone witless.'

'That wasn't nice,' agreed Dad, as he buttered a second piece of toast.

'Most of the girls thought the ghost bit was brilliant,'

said Flame. 'It'll give them all something to talk about for ages. Lisha will never stop yattering on about it. Pia's pretty philosophical – she won't let it worry her for long – and Janey's pretty robust. The only person who was really shaky was Katie – and even she was laughing about it later. The other girls didn't see the ghost, so they weren't too frightened.'

'Well, let's hope so,' said Dad.

'They'll all want another Sprite Towers Hallowe'en party next year, of course,' said Marina. 'And *everyone* will want to come next time!'

'Perhaps we could do ghost tours around Sprite Towers,' mused Dad. '"Meet the ghost in the towers" – that sort of thing. Probably make a killing. What do you think, Ottalie? Shall we start a new business?'

Mum laughed. 'You can, by all means, love – but I'm sticking to teaching music. I'm not very fond of ghosts.'

'Everybody will be talking about the ghost at school today,' said Ariel, pushing back her fluffy blond hair.

'It's a good story – to be able to say, "I was there",' said Marina. 'Only we know how frightening the ghost really is.'

'That's true,' agreed Mum.

'Since we were on the telly about the monster slug invasion at Sprite Towers, everyone thinks the Sprite family are a weird lot anyway!' laughed Ash.

'This will confirm their suspicions,' grinned Dad. He took another sip of coffee, then said, 'Well, I never wanted to be like everybody else – and I hope you girls don't grow up wanting to be, either.'

Flame grinned and looked around at her sisters. 'I don't think you need to worry about that, Dad.'

Marina, Ash and Ariel caught her eye and laughed.

'I think you should collect us from school dressed as a zombie doctor, Dad,' said Ariel. 'That would give people something to talk about.'

'There are limits,' laughed Mum.

'So, what do you want us to say to people about the ghost?' Flame turned from her father to her mother.

Mum looked thoughtful. Then she said, 'I think you should all say that we don't know what it is.'

'What if people ask if we've seen it before?' asked Ash.

'Then say we've seen it once or twice,' said Dad.

'Play it down, girls, please,' said Mum, firmly. 'We don't want the parents of the girls worrying.'

'Nor do we want any more reporters turning up,' muttered Dad. 'Or people who want to come and record the ghost and snoop about measuring things. I hope the story doesn't get picked up by the papers . . .'

'No reason why it should, love,' said Mum, reassuringly. 'It was the scientist who found the slugs who alerted the press last time, remember?'

'Hm,' said Dad, rather gloomily.

'You like a quiet life, don't you, Dad?' said Ash, smiling at her father.

'Well, I can't stand a lot of fuss,' he agreed, with a twinkle in his eye. 'And I've more than enough noise from you lot!'

Sure enough, at school the sisters were bombarded by questions about the ghost at Sprite Towers. Everyone wanted to know about it.

Alex and Bill, the Tolver twins, were particularly interested as they were always looking for new tricks. They hung around Marina, who they both liked, but she side-stepped all their questions about the haunting of Sprite Towers.

'I've never trusted you two since you put the monster slugs in the garden as a joke,' she grinned.

'Very wise,' laughed Alex, kicking the gravel.

'Oh, come on, Marina – tell us about the ghost!' said Bill.

'No, I'm not saying a word,' she said with a laugh – and she walked off.

All over Drysdale's School, the matter of the Sprites' ghost took on an air of mystery and amusement. Everyone was intrigued. Marina, Ash and Ariel said little, but played along. Flame only smiled, quietly; her mind was on other things.

We must go into the portal soon, she said to herself. Margaret is getting stronger by the day.

In her mind, she churned this thought over and over.

I don't feel ready, she thought. I still haven't worked out the significance of the photographs and what we need to take. I don't have the missing piece. What do we do when we get into the portal? Where will it take us? What happens if we cannot find Margaret? Or what if she attacks us? And how will we get back?

Flame Sprite struggled with these questions. As the eldest sister, she felt responsible for her younger sisters, who usually relied on her ability to form a strategy. What if I get it all wrong, she wondered. What then?

Her mood was anxious as she pondered these issues. By contrast, her sisters put the matter of what lay ahead to one side and were amused by the fuss about the ghost.

'Flame, what's the matter?' asked Pia, after lunch. 'All morning you've looked deep in thought. What's on your mind?'

What do I say? Flame thought. I can't tell my best friend about my magic powers. Nobody must ever know. Besides, she'd never believe me if I told her my sisters and I were about to go into a portal . . .

Flame turned to Pia and smiled. 'Sorry – I'm just a bit tired after the party.'

When she saw Verena – they came face to face in the corridor – the two girls looked hard at each other. Not warily, as they might once have done: more with a germ of mutual respect.

There's something different about Verena, thought Flame. There's a new look in her eyes . . .

But, with the matter of the portal pressing, Flame soon forgot about Verena.

That night, Marina, Ash and Ariel sat on Flame's bed.

'Do we *have* to go into the portal?' asked Ariel.

'Is it really the only way to stop Margaret's ghost?' asked Ash, her brown eyes troubled.

'I feel ever so frightened . . .' said Ariel, hugging her knees.

'We mustn't let the ghost take Archie again – she might not bring him back next time,' said Ash.

'That's true,' agreed Ariel, and she sighed heavily. 'Oh
dear . . .'

The four girls sat with glum faces.

'So what's the plan, Flame?' asked Marina.

Flame swallowed hard. 'Well – I'm still working on that.'

Ash sensed her sister's hesitance. 'I'm sure you'll come up
with something – you always do.'

Her elder sister gave a nervous smile. 'I hope so,' she said,
very softly.

'What is it that you're looking for?' asked Marina.

'It's this link – the thing that connects the photograph.'

'Which photograph? I thought there were two you were
looking at,' said Marina.

'There's the one of Lily and Arthur and their children,'
said Flame. 'Then there's the one of Violet Duggery with
George and Fred.'

She stopped, bit her lip. 'I wonder why I said "the photograph"?'

'Perhaps there's another one – something you haven't
found yet,' suggested Ariel.

Flame looked into her little sister's big grey eyes, a new
thought suddenly forming in her mind. Ariel often sent them
thinking on a new tack, and Flame sensed this might be one
of those occasions. 'I'll have another look,' she said. 'Thank
you, Ariel.'

'We'll leave you to it,' said Marina. 'We'd better get some
sleep.'

A few minutes later, Marina, Ash and Ariel drifted off to
sleep in their beds. Flame sat with the box of photographs on

her red duvet. Beside the bed, on the little table, were the two old black and white photographs of Lily and Arthur and their children, and the one of Violet, George and Fred.

Is there another photograph in the box that I might have missed, she wondered. She stared at the box. Yes, she thought. There's something else. I can feel it . . .

She opened the lid and looked into the box. Inside were around a hundred photographs.

How should I do this? she wondered. I could spread them all out again and go through them, one by one. Or I can do this differently . . .

She frowned. If I put the photographs out and look at them, I will be using my logical mind to decide, she thought. Somehow, I know that's not the way I need to do this . . .

Her face cleared. I know what I must do, she decided. I must use my *power* to find the solution to this problem. I'll do it another way.

Flame closed her eyes and began to breathe deeply and steadily. I call on my power of the East to help me, she thought. I call on the power of the East to help me see and find what it is I need to take with us in the portal.

When her mind felt calm and completely focused, and with her eyes still closed, she reached into the box of photographs with her left hand.

She moved her fingers through the pile of photographs, shuffling them this way, then that, burrowing deeper. Where is it? she thought, moving her hand through the images. Where is the photograph I am looking for?

Then, suddenly, she gripped her fingers tight.

It's this one, she thought. Whatever this image is – that's the one I am looking for.

Holding her breath, she drew out the photograph very carefully. By the light of her bedside lamp, she examined a small, very old, black and white photograph of two children.

A girl – about ten years old, Flame guessed – was sitting on a chair, looking at the camera. Beside her stood a boy, who looked a bit younger – probably about eight years old.

The girl was smiling – a slightly mysterious smile, thought Flame. She had dark eyes and long, thick dark hair, which was drawn behind her head, then hung down her back. Across her forehead was a fringe. Her dress was dark-coloured velvet, with a round, lacy collar and long sleeves. The top half of the dress was highly decorated, with ruches and ruffles. Around her waist was a wide silk sash of a paler colour. On her feet, she wore black ankle boots that buttoned up the sides. She looks very smartly dressed, thought Flame.

And another thing, she noted. The girl's left hand is resting in the boy's right hand. The two are connected, she thought.

The boy was looking at the girl. His right arm lay across the top of her shoulder and he was smiling at her. He looks as if he really loves her, thought Flame.

She looked at the boy's clothes: he wore a grey tweed suit, with short trousers that finished just under his knees. His jacket was short and finished with buttons and braid. Under this, he wore a waistcoat and a pale-coloured shirt. Like the girl, he wore short, black ankle boots. The boy's hair was fair – much lighter than the girl's. His eyes, too, looked lighter, she thought.

So who are they, she wondered, this girl and boy? And why have I picked this photograph? Funny, I don't remember seeing this one before. If I can work out the date this was taken, I could work out who these children are ...

She glanced over at her bookcase on the other side of the room and got out of bed. A few seconds later, she was back, a big colourful book on historical costume spread out on her lap. She flicked through till she found illustrations of children wearing the same type of clothes as those in the photographs. The date here is the 1870s, she thought. So which Sprites would have been about ten and eight around that time? It couldn't have been Lily and Arthur, as they'd be forty-something: I remember Charles Smythson telling me Arthur was born in 1830, when he was researching the family portraits.

She picked up the photo again. Maybe these are two of Arthur and Lily's children? When did Sidney die? Ah, yes, she remembered, I'm sure Grandma told me he died in 1958, in his late eighties. So, how old would he have been in 1870?

Grabbing a pen and paper from her bedside table, she started to do some sums. If Sidney was born around 1865, she calculated, he'd be around eight years old in 1873. That would fit, she thought, picking up the photograph once more.

And the older girl? Could it be Margaret Sprite, Sidney's elder sister? Grandma told me she was a couple of years older than Sidney, she thought.

She looked hard at the photograph for a long time. I'm looking at a photograph of Sidney and Margaret together as children, she thought. I *know* it. And the one thing that really strikes me is that I can see these two children really *love* each other . . .

Flame sighed long and hard. This is it, she thought. I'm sure I have the thing George told me to find. I know what the connection is. I have the missing bit of our plan. Now I must sleep, for tomorrow we must go into the portal and meet with Margaret Sprite. I'll tell my sisters in the morning.

She took a last look at the photograph of the two children, then put it, carefully, on her bedside table. She placed the lid back on the box and laid it on the floor, along with the pad and pen. A minute after she had switched out the light and snuggled down under the duvet, Flame Sprite fell into a deep sleep.

Over at The Oaks, Verena Glass was lying in her bed, thinking. She was tired after the party the night before, but her mind would not switch off. Round and round it went, as she kept returning to the image of Flame Sprite standing in the shadows, watching her with the ghost. Then, catching Flame's eye as the ghost terrified the girls in the cupboard.

Her thoughts turned to her grandmother, Glenda. She thought about all the questions her grandmother had asked her, and how she had gone on and on and on in her quest for information.

Why *is* Grandma so obsessed with the Sprites? she wondered. What is this all *really* about? There's a lot that Grandma has not told me – I know very little.

The story of how Margaret Sprite had lost her house, and how Sidney had banished her from Sprite Towers, was awful

– and it made her feel angry. But, at the same time, Verena realised that she had only heard the story from her grandmother's point of view – and that there may be another. It's only my grandmother who says Sidney Sprite was a bad man. Nobody else says it.

The ghost seemed friendly to me – but it wasn't to the other girls. Flame knew what was happening – and she was surprised, thought Verena. It was as if Flame saw something in me – something I have not yet seen in myself. There's something Flame knows, she thought.

As her mind began to settle, the darkness closed in. A moment later, Verena was asleep.

Downstairs at The Oaks, Glenda paced about, restlessly.

What's next? she wondered. The girls will try to get rid of the ghost. How will they try to do that?

A thought struck her. Charles told me that the Sprite Sisters opened the portal: what if they opened it to look for Margaret – and she attacked them? Or trapped them?

Glenda smiled. That would be a quick way to get rid of them, she thought. Lure them in – and lose them somewhere in time. Ha!

And if the Sprite Sisters were lost, Glenda considered, Marilyn Sprite would be distracted and would probably get off the trail of her missing money – if that's what she's been doing in the south of France. That would be welcome, too: Marilyn must *not* find the money. No one must ever know about that . . .

Glenda sat down on the cream silk sofa and crossed her

long dancer's legs. Then she smoothed back her pale blond hair and closed her eyes.

I must find out what is going on, she thought. And she turned her mind inwards and breathed deeply, focusing on Margaret Sprite – trying to sense her.

Then, in her mind, she saw a rainbow of light. It's what Charles told me – the rainbow of light that is the entrance to the portal.

Margaret, she called to the spirit of her grandmother. We must trap the Sprite Sisters in the portal! We must let not them come back!

Then she asked, 'When will it be?'

When the answer came, she said softly, 'I will help you, Grandmother. I will be there to help you take the Sprite Sisters far away and make sure they do not ever come back.'

CHAPTER FIFTEEN

DANGER!

IT WAS ten o'clock on Friday evening. In his smart London flat, Charles Smythson dropped the Sprite Towers portrait inventory into his open briefcase and shut the lid. The job was complete – and he was pleased with the result. Tomorrow morning, he would give it to Colin and Ottalie Sprite.

He was nervous, yes, of returning to the house and meeting again with the family. Colin and Ottalie remained close, but the girls and their grandmother knew him to have bad magic and to have worked for Glenda Glass. They knew he had betrayed their secrets – had exposed them to Glenda's scrutiny and possible further danger.

What they would not know, when he walked through the door of Sprite Towers, was that he had been true to his word and broken free of Glenda. It would take time to build their trust, and, now, just as he had a chance to start, Glenda was at his throat once again.

Getting Marilyn Sprite and her granddaughters' respect was one thing. Harder than this would be getting Glenda to believe him and leave him alone. He was under no illusion of the challenge that lay ahead in convincing her that *that was it*. He was not going to do any more of her dirty work. Nor would he harm his distant cousins, the Sprite Sisters. He would tell Glenda this weekend. And that, he hoped, would be an end to it.

With his bag packed and his briefcase ready, Charles sat down to watch television. For the next hour, he relaxed and wound down from the busy week.

When the phone rang, he hesitated, wondering who might be trying to reach him at this late hour.

'Charles,' barked Glenda Glass, as he answered.

'Hello,' said Charles, noting her lack of greeting.

'There have been developments.'

Charles sank back into his chair and sighed. 'No, Glenda – no more,' he said, in a firm voice. 'I'm not interested.'

Glenda laughed a cold laugh. 'So you don't want to know what I have planned for the Sprite Sisters?'

A chill ran down Charles's back. He rubbed his hand across his face, anxiously.

'The ghost of my grandmother, Margaret – your great-grandmother has been making a dreadful nuisance of herself at Sprite Towers,' continued Glenda. 'The family would like to be shot of her, but I think I can safely say that it is the

Sprite Sisters who will be going away – and on a *very* long trip.'

Charles sat forward in his seat. His mouth felt dry. What's she going to do? he wondered. Where are the girls going?

Glenda ignored his silence. 'Now, I expect to see you tomorrow, Charles. We have a lot to discuss, you and I.' And she put down the phone.

Charles breathed out heavily and stared across the room. His mind flashed back to the last time he saw the sisters, in August. Ariel and he had got pulled into the portal, but George Sprite had brought them out. Thank heavens George helped us, he thought.

But what were the girls up against now? Glenda had talked of 'dark forces under the earth' when she called him last week. Ottalie had told him about the aquifer under the lawn, when they talked on the phone. What was happening at Sprite Towers?

Charles drew a sharp breath and felt his heart begin to race. He had the sudden intuition that the girls were in immediate danger. What would they do to rid themselves of a malevolent ghost in the house, he wondered. Might they go into the portal? Was that Glenda's idea of a 'long trip'?

Who will help them? he asked himself. Their grandmother is away. They may not know that Glenda is using her power to help Margaret Sprite.

Another chilling thought struck him.

What if the girls are planning to open the portal tonight? And, what if Glenda traps them in the portal?

He jumped up with a mounting sense of panic and looked

at his watch. Nearly eleven o'clock. What shall I do? Shall I call them? No, too late now – they'll be in bed. And how would I explain this to Colin or Ottalie? Shall I go tomorrow morning, as planned?

No, he thought, it'll be too late. I can feel something's wrong. It'll take me three hours to get there. If I leave now, I might just be able to stop them . . .

Grabbing his jacket, briefcase and overnight bag, Charles switched off the lights, walked out of the flat and slammed the door behind him.

Outside, on the busy London street, he opened the car door and threw in the jacket and bags. A moment later, he turned on the engine and swung the car out on to the road.

Just before midnight, Mum walked up the wide mahogany staircase to the second floor. There, she quietly opened the door to each of her daughter's rooms and checked that all was well. Downstairs, Dad took Bert and Archie outside for a few minutes, then came in, settled the dogs and checked the doors were all locked. He was coming up the stairs, as Mum came down from the girls' rooms. Then they went into their bedroom on the first floor and settled down for the night.

Soon after, all was quiet at Sprite Towers – but not for long.

At two a.m., Flame's alarm beeped beside her head. She grabbed it, then fumbled to turn on her bedside lamp and sat up, blearily. What am I doing? Ah yes – the portal.

Shivering slightly, she got up and pulled on her clothes. Better put on a thick jumper and socks, she thought. It'll be cold up there in the tower. Then she strapped her watch around her wrist.

What else? The photo. I mustn't forget the photo. She picked up the photograph of the two children that she had been scrutinising before and pushed it into her jeans pocket.

And the plan and the letter, she thought – I must take them as well. And she stuffed those in, too.

Flame looked around her room. I hope we will soon be safely back in our beds, she thought. I hope we are doing the right thing . . .

For a few seconds she stood there. Doubt crept up on her. We don't *have* to go into the portal, she thought. There may be another way to stop Margaret. Perhaps I should just leave my sisters sleeping . . .

Somewhere, deep in her mind, she heard a woman laughing. It was a cold, cruel laugh. I've heard that laugh before, thought Flame. I've heard Glenda Glass laugh like that – and Margaret laughs like that, too.

But Flame Sprite was not one to dither when something needed to be done. Despite her misgivings, she wanted to act, to rid the house of the malevolent spirit that had been frightening them.

Resolve, she decided. Resolve.

As she stood there in the dark, a face flashed into her mind: Mrs Duggery, in her lilac knitted hat. Mrs Duggery! Of course, thought Flame, why didn't I think of her before? And for a minute she stood, her eyes closed, telling the magical old lady what was happening. Wherever you are, Mrs Duggery, we may need your help tonight.

Holding the image of Mrs Duggery in her mind, she

turned off the light and crept along the corridor to rouse her sisters. She had told them that morning that tonight they would go into the portal. Ten minutes later, Marina, Ash and Ariel were dressed in jeans and sweaters and ready to go.

'You sure you'll all be warm enough?' whispered Flame. 'It'll be cold in the Tower Room.'

'Yes, stop fussing,' hissed Marina.

'Okay, let's go.'

Ariel gulped. 'I'm frightened,' she said, her grey eyes anxious. Flame put her arm around her little sister's shoulders.

'We stick together,' said Flame. 'Remember – we must stick together.'

Ariel nodded.

Then the sisters crept upstairs to the West Tower.

Nearly there, thought Charles Smythson, as he raced along the country roads towards Sprite Towers. He glanced at the clock on the dashboard. Should be there by two-thirty, he thought. Better leave the car on the driveway up to the house and walk the rest of the way. Don't want to disturb anybody – especially the dogs.

How am I going to get in? he wondered. Here am I, racing to help the Sprite Sisters – and I'm not sure I shall even be able to get into the house . . .

He turned into the long driveway of Sprite Towers and stopped the car about halfway down. Then he got out, shut the door quietly, locked it, and began to walk towards the house. It's a dark night – no moon, he thought, peering up to the inky sky.

A minute later, the huge red-brick house loomed in front of him in the darkness. Better go round to the back, he thought, walking on to the lawn. However am I going to get in? Colin locks all the doors at night . . .

Perhaps I can get in through the conservatory, he thought. Maybe Colin forgot about that door . . .

He walked carefully over the grass around the west side of the house. As he rounded the corner, he just made out the shape of a bicycle propped up against the wall. He moved closer. Funny bike – looks like an old boneshaker, he thought, staring at it through the darkness. Then he moved on.

The dogs, thought Charles, as he crept past the kitchen door – for he'd heard about the new puppy. Mustn't wake the dogs . . .

He reached the conservatory door – and stopped. What am I doing? he thought. I must be mad!

For a few seconds, he stood there, his hands in his pockets, wondering whether to abandon this venture.

It's crazy, he thought. The girls are probably fast asleep and perfectly safe. Glenda was probably just winding me up. If Colin and Ottalie find me creeping about their house at this time of night, they'll wonder what on earth is going on. Oh Lord . . .

What to do? He rubbed his hand over his chin and breathed out hard.

The memory of Glenda Glass's voice on the phone galvanised him. I might as well just try the conservatory door, now that I'm here, he thought. And he grabbed the handle.

It turned in his hand – and he pushed open the door.

Charles stared at the open glass door. How strange, he thought. Why would Colin have left this door open?

A few seconds later, he was standing in the hallway. Silently, he took off his shoes and began to climb the wide mahogany staircase up to the West Tower.

Meanwhile, at The Oaks, Glenda Glass pulled on a black coat and hat. Silently, she grabbed her gloves and car keys, then opened the back door and let herself out of the house. She walked lightly over the gravel to her silver car and climbed in, shutting the door gently behind her. As soon as the engine was turned on, she pulled away swiftly and quietly.

Her eyes glinted and her mouth set in a thin cruel line as she sped along the country lanes. As she pulled into the driveway of Sprite Towers and saw Charles's car in the headlights, Glenda exploded with anger.

What? He's already here! She growled, getting out of the car and closing the door quietly. He must have come to help the girls. He'll pay for this. I will make Charles pay for this . . .

For a moment, Glenda stood in the darkness and let her eyes adjust. Soon, she could make out shapes of trees. There was the house in front of her. Walking on the grass, she moved quickly around the west side of the house, noticing a big, old bicycle propped up against the wall.

She walked on, over the lawn – then stopped and looked along the length of the house.

I can't see Charles, she thought, peering into the dark. He must have got into the house.

Which door did he get in? The kitchen? No, they've got dogs in there, she thought. The conservatory? I'll try that.

The last time I tried to get into Sprite Towers, I failed, remembered Glenda. But I won't fail again. I *have* to get to the tower tonight.

She walked softly towards the glass door of the conservatory and reached for the handle.

It did not turn. Damn, it's locked, thought Glenda. She let go. I'll have to use my magic power to open it, she thought, stepping back.

She was just about to lift her hand and point her finger at the handle, when she had the sensation that someone was behind her – that someone was watching her.

She turned around, scanning the darkness. Who's there? she wondered.

Charles? It must be Charles.

Then her eyes made out a shape. Someone was standing on the lawn about ten metres away.

Glenda drew a sharp breath. The shape moved forward through the darkness.

It doesn't look like Charles, thought Glenda.

Her heart quickened. She stood back against the door, hoping whoever was walking towards her might miss her.

But the figure walked straight towards her – and stopped a few paces away.

Glenda Glass looked at the tiny, very old lady standing in front of her. She had piercing eyes and a face that was as wrinkled as a walnut. On her head was a lilac knitted hat and on her feet, big brown boots.

'Mrs Duggery,' said Glenda, with a snort of derision.

Mrs Duggery was silent. Her eyes glinted.

Glenda waited. Should she try to use her power?

Then Mrs Duggery said, in a sharp voice, 'Time you left these 'ere people alone, Glenda Glass. You an' Margaret – yer done enough damage.'

It wasn't a request: it was a command.

Glenda sized up the tiny, old woman. Surely her power has withered at her age, she thought, drawing herself up. And she raised her right hand.

Mrs Duggery was faster.

As Glenda pointed her finger, a massive bolt of power shot past her head. It did not hit her, but Glenda reeled, disorientated.

Mrs Duggery dropped her hand and watched, silent.

Then she said, in her broad Norfolk accent, 'That wer' a warnin'. If yer want ter get ter the Sproites, Glenda, first yer'l hav' ter get pas' me.'

In the West Tower room, the four Sprite Sisters were beginning to build the magical light to create the portal. Flame sat, cross-legged with her back against the wall, at the east side of the circular room. Marina sat at the south, Ash at the west and Ariel at the north. Their eyes were closed, their hands lifted slightly with their palms open towards the centre of the circle. As they focused their minds, the tower room began to fill with bright blue light. At the same time, the noise of the wind outside, the creaks in the house, even the sound of their own breathing, began to recede. All was silent.

'Direct your power to the centre,' said Flame. 'Hold it steady. Remember the balance: it's the balance between our four powers, Air, Water, Earth and Fire – North, South, West and East – which keeps our magic strong.'

As their powers connected and grew stronger, the colours of the rainbow began to pulse through the room in waves of light: red, orange, yellow, green, blue and violet.

'The energy is building!' cried Flame. 'Hold the power!'

Second by second, the rainbow light grew more radiant. Brighter waves of colour filled the room. Then, suddenly, the light began to contract and curve into an arc of rainbow light. The arc stretched from the centre of the wooden floorboards and seemed to pierce the wall, high up on the West Tower.

'Open your eyes!' cried Flame.

Then, as if the Sprite Sisters were of one mind, they stood up and moved towards the west wall.

The rainbow of light shone on to the centre of the floor. As the girls moved closer together, a band of white light appeared in the middle of the rainbow. Moment by moment, the white light got brighter.

'It's coming,' whispered Flame. 'Now, listen carefully. Once we're in the portal, we stick together like glue. Margaret Sprite is waiting for us, so be awake – be ready.'

A set of steps began to form in the white arc of light.

'The bridge of light!' exclaimed Marina, looking up at it in awe.

Flame said, 'Now hold together! Don't let go!' The four Sprite Sisters gripped each other's hands as tightly as they could and moved towards the steps.

In a commanding voice, Flame cried up towards the light, *'We seek Margaret Sprite in the year 1910!'* She put her foot on to the bottom step, her face radiant in the white arc of light.

Marina, Ash and Ariel followed, and step by step the four girls moved forward.

As soon as they were all standing on the bridge of light, the rainbow and white light began to spin around them. Slowly it went at first, as they inched up the steps – then faster and faster until everything became a blur.

For what felt like an eternity, the Sprite Sisters seemed to spin and whirl, round and round, desperately trying to hold on to one another as they hurtled along the tunnel of light.

And, then, suddenly, everything went still.

CHAPTER SIXTEEN

MARGARET'S PARLOUR

'WHERE ARE we?' whispered Ariel.

The Sprite Sisters stood close together, their legs shaky and their heads still spinning. They blinked and looked around them.

They were standing at the back of a dark, sparsely furnished room. On the other side of the room, a small coal fire burned in the grate. On the left of the fireplace was an armchair with a high back. On the right side of the fire were two wooden chairs. A small rug covered the bare wooden floorboards in front of the fire. The walls were covered with a faded floral paper and in front of the window hung tatty crimson curtains. On the side wall, a gas lamp hissed and gave out a dull glow.

'I think it may be Margaret Sprite's parlour. We're in the

house she moved to when her husband died,' whispered Flame. 'It looks very shabby.'

'What time are we in?' asked Ash.

'Around 1910,' whispered Flame.

Marina stared at the small fire. 'It's cold in here.'

'So what do we do now?' whispered Ariel, nervously.

'We wait,' said Flame.

The girls gazed around the room.

Flame started, and fixed her eyes on the high-backed armchair beside the fire. This was turned away from them, towards the fire.

Marina, Ash and Ariel followed Flame's gaze, registered its intensity.

Ariel gesticulated with her hand, as if to say, 'There's someone sitting in the armchair.'

Flame nodded, put her hand out to stop Ariel moving forward. Then she mouthed, 'Stay together.'

The girls huddled closer. Their hearts pumped faster and faster. All eyes were on the armchair by the fire.

Then a voice rose from behind the chair – a woman's voice, a cold voice with a rasping edge to it. 'Come here. Let me see you.'

Marina, Ash and Ariel looked at Flame, their eyes wide.

Flame shook her head. 'Wait,' she whispered. She braced herself, then said in a bold voice, 'Show yourself!'

Marina, Ash and Ariel looked at Flame, then back at the chair, in horror, as a voice laughed. It was the same cackling laughter they had heard at Sprite Towers. The Sprite Sisters gulped and shivered in fear.

'Margaret Sprite, show yourself!' demanded Flame.

Ariel thought her heart would burst through her chest, it was pumping so hard. She clutched Marina tight.

The figure in the chair stood up and turned towards them. The Sprite Sisters gasped.

'So, you think my parlour is shabby.' Margaret Sprite's voice was like thick honey. 'And who are you, to be standing in my house?'

'We are Sidney Sprite's great-great-granddaughters,' said Flame, in a hesitant voice.

Margaret Sprite gave a low growl, as she moved towards them. A tall woman – much taller than the sisters had expected – she seemed to hover over them. 'Oh, so you have come back through time,' she said. 'Then you must have the Sprite magic.' She peered down at Flame and hissed, 'If I'd been allowed to live at Sprite Towers, I should have been a great deal more comfortable.'

Flame was speechless. Her sisters huddled so close they could feel one another's hearts beating.

Margaret Sprite's eyes were dark and her mouth was thin and cruel. She wore a long black dress with a high neck and ruffles all the way down the front. Her skirt cascaded to the ground in folds. Her thick, dark hair was piled on to her head in an Edwardian style.

She held out her hand to Flame. 'You have come with the secret plan – I can *feel* it close by. *Give it to me.*'

Flame's jaw set. 'No,' she said, shaking her head.

Margaret gave a sharp laugh, then turned and waved her hand towards the fire. 'Why don't we all sit down . . .'

Marina, Ash and Ariel looked at Flame. Flame nodded. The four sisters moved, gingerly, to the two chairs by the fireside. Flame and Ariel sat on one, side by side; Marina and Ash squashed on to the other. Margaret sat down opposite, on the high-backed armchair.

'Is there anybody else here?' asked Ariel, suddenly.

Margaret fixed the youngest Sprite sister with her glittering dark eyes. 'No,' she said. 'Who were you expecting?'

'No one,' gulped Ariel, tightening her grip on Flame's hand.

Margaret turned her gaze, once again, to Flame. 'You look as if you have a strong spirit.'

'Yes,' said Flame, with an air of defiance. She looked into Margaret's eyes, determined not to let this woman beat her down. 'You broke the Sprite Code of Honour!'

Margaret laughed a chilling laugh. 'And you, young lady, will lose your power if you try to hurt me. So-called "good" Sprites who believe in the Code always lose their power when they try to hurt other Sprites.'

Flame gasped. 'I shall only use my magic for good!'

'Ha!' sneered Margaret. For a few seconds, she stared at Flame. Then she said, 'We'll see.'

A sense of panic began to creep over Flame. How would they get out of this room without losing their power? Would they get out of this room at all?

Margaret noted the sudden fear in Flame's eyes and hissed, 'It's only we "other" Sprites – the ones you prissy little girls would call "bad" – who have *real* magic power.'

Flame's fear turned to anger. 'What rubbish! How can

'anything bad be better than something good?'

'You are not deferential,' said Margaret. 'Have your parents not taught you never to contradict your elders? Manners must have changed. The young are less polite, I think, in your time.'

Flame looked away, towards the fire. Stay cool, she thought, clenching her fist into a tight ball. Don't react, or I'll lose my temper and get distracted.

Margaret watched her like a hawk. Marina, Ash and Ariel waited, hardly daring to draw breath.

But it was too much for Flame. Her green eyes blazing, she turned to Margaret and spat out, '*Why* are you trying to hurt our family?'

Margaret gave a chilling smile. Marina, Ash and Ariel gasped.

'Flame, no!' whispered Ash.

But Flame was not listening. She wanted to know the truth. 'Why do you blame Sidney for your misfortune?'

'Because he is responsible.' Margaret's voice was cold and flat. She paused for a second, then said, 'I only want what is rightly mine.'

'And what is that?' asked Flame.

'The secret, and Sprite Towers, of course.'

Flame's voice rose with indignation. 'Sidney Sprite paid you handsomely for the land at Sprite Towers. The house belongs to our branch of the family now. And, if your mother, Lily, chose to give the secret to Sidney, then it is not rightfully yours. That, also, belonged to Sidney – and now to us.'

Margaret gave another low growl. Ariel gave a little cry.

Suddenly, Flame jumped out of her seat and stood in front of the fire. '*He loved you!*' she shouted at Margaret. '*Your brother loved you! And you loved him! I've seen it! I have proof!*'

With a roar of rage, Margaret jumped up from her chair and the two Sprites faced each other. Their eyes locked as they began to turn on the wooden floor, like wrestlers circling each other.

'*Give – me – the – plan!*' growled Margaret.

Marina, Ash and Ariel jumped off their chairs, but where to stand? There was no space on the floor, close to Flame. The two Sprites were moving round, eyeball to eyeball. The sisters glanced at one another, wondering whether to use their magic powers – but realised if they tried, they might hit Flame instead of Margaret.

Flame's face was red with passion as she shouted, 'Sidney would not have hurt you – but you were bad and unkind!'

Margaret roared as she raised both her hands over Flame's head. In a split second, a huge bolt of power shot out of her fingers, sending Flame reeling to the floor. Marina, Ash and Ariel screamed, '*Flame!*'

'*Give me the secret plan!*' hissed Margaret, leaning down over Flame.

Flame lay stunned, inert. Her head pounded. What's happening? Where am I?

Margaret watched the copper-haired girl as she grabbed the seat of the high-backed chair and began to pull herself up very slowly, her face contorted in pain.

'Give me the plan!' hissed Margaret again, holding out her

hand to receive it.

Slowly, Flame pulled herself up to a sitting position. Then, staring down at the floor, she shook her head. 'No,' she said, and drooped slightly.

Looming above her, Margaret's voice was loud, cold, deliberate. 'GIVE ME THE PLAN.'

Flame reached into her jeans pocket. Her fingers fumbled, as her head still spun. The photograph, she thought. I must show Margaret the photograph . . .

Marina gasped and moved forwards. 'No, Flame – don't give it to her!' she cried. 'Don't give her the plan!'

Margaret turned, putting up her hand to stop Marina reaching her sister. 'Quiet, *you*!' she hissed.

Marina gasped, transfixed by the power in Margaret's eyes.

Ash grabbed Marina's arm. 'Wait!' she whispered, pulling her back. At the same time, Ariel moved to Marina's side.

With a harsh laugh, Margaret – now turned away from Flame – looked down at her sisters. 'And what do *you* three propose to do?'

Ariel gasped with outrage. 'You are a *wicked* woman!'

'You stole our puppy!' cried Ash.

'And you frightened our family and friends – *you evil hag!*' shouted Marina.

Margaret peered down at Marina and laughed again. 'Dear oh, dear! And just what are you going to do about it?'

Those few seconds that Margaret was being distracted by her sisters gave Flame time to act. Still fumbling for the photograph in her pocket, she had glanced up and realised

Margaret's back was turned towards her. Now, clenching her jaw, she lifted her hand and let out a flash of magic power. Like a bolt of lightning, her power of Fire crackled around Margaret's head.

The older woman cried out and grabbed her head. As she reeled sideways, Marina, Ash and Ariel rushed to Flame and pulled her up from the floor.

By the time Margaret turned, the four Sprite Sisters stood together and faced her across the floor.

Then Margaret really let rip.

With a great howl of rage, she raised her hands. Huge flashes of dark power surged out of her fingers, sending the four Sprite Sisters spinning backwards.

'*This is my last warning!*' roared Margaret. '*Or there'll be worse than that!*'

Marina, Ash and Ariel lay on the floor, holding their heads and writhing with pain.

'I can't see anything!' screamed Ariel, blinded by the light.

Marina grabbed her. 'It's okay, Ariel,' she cried. 'I'm here.' Beside her, Ash moaned and held her hands across her face.

Margaret looked down at Flame, who lay with her face on the rug, her eyes closed, her arms stretched out in front of her. She was holding something between her fingers.

Margaret Sprite reached down and grasped it. 'The plan!' she hissed.

It was not what Margaret was expecting.

Instead, she stared at an old photograph – a photograph of herself and her brother as young children. She covered her mouth with her hand, to stifle a cry, and sank into the high-backed chair. All the time, her eyes were fixed on the image of the two children.

Somewhere, far back in time, a memory surfaced. Margaret Sprite remembered something – and a little chink opened in her cold heart.

As she sat, completely absorbed by this photograph, she forgot about the four girls in her sitting room. She was remembering something long forgotten: love – her brother's love.

In her mind, she heard laughter, she saw Sidney and herself playing together – looking for tadpoles in the pond, racing over the lawn, spinning their tops, decorating the Christmas tree with their mother, Lily. Childhood memories crowded into her mind. Sidney and I had such fun together, she thought. We were so close. There was such love between us.

She began to remember how, as young adults, she and Sidney had found their magic powers and how they had to learn to master them. We both had powerful magic, she thought. Sidney always wanted to use his magic power for good.

She thought back to the day that she found the dark magic and remembered how it changed everything between them. She had enjoyed the feeling it had given her when she realised she could manipulate people and make them do things against their will. It amused her to think that she could erase people's memories. She liked the feeling of control. It made her feel important and strong – and that sense of powerfulness became more important to her than anything.

She remembered how Sidney had begged her not to play

with the dark magic, but she did not listen. Still he begged her – but she stopped hearing his pleas, drawn further and further into her new world of manipulation and fear.

She remembered her fury when her mother, Lily, gave the 'secret' to Sidney. She was seething, but still Sidney loved her and tried to help her. And, when her husband, Thomas, lost all their money, it was Sidney who came forward and offered to buy their house and land. He paid Thomas a lot of money for it – but Thomas lost all that, too.

And when Thomas died and she was left looking after her two children alone, with very little money, Sidney tried to help, but she was angry and jealous, and as her anger towards her brother increased, her dark power grew stronger.

Things got worse – she even caused an accident to hurt Sidney. After that, he said, 'Enough', but she could see the pain in his eyes when he told her she must no longer come to Sprite Towers. It went against every fibre of his being to say that to his once-dear sister, but she had pushed him too far.

Now, sitting in her cold parlour, Margaret stared at the fire burning in the grate. She stared and stared, as one memory after another came to her mind. Where did the love go, she wondered. What happened to those happy years?

She held up the photograph and gazed at it again. A feeling of warmth began to pass over her body, as her heart began to open. The love is still there, she thought. The love never dies. It's been there all the time – only I haven't seen it, haven't felt it till now . . .

So intense was this feeling of love and remembered happiness, that Margaret did not notice the four Sprite Sisters pick themselves up, slowly and carefully. As she gazed at the photograph in her fingers, she did not hear, as the girls crept quietly behind the high-backed armchair and out of the parlour. And, if she had heard them, she would have let them pass – these great-great-granddaughters of her brother.

As Flame reached the door, she glanced back at Margaret. All she can see is the photograph, she thought. All she can feel are the memories. She has forgotten we are here. The photograph has triggered a feeling so deep that, at last, Margaret can feel the healing power of her brother's love.

She will not hurt us now, thought Flame, as she closed the door quietly behind them.

CHAPTER SEVENTEEN

THE
ESCAPE

THEY WERE standing in a dark, narrow hallway that led from the front to the back of the old house. At one side, rickety wooden stairs led up to bedrooms.

The house was silent, apart from the tick-tock of a grandfather clock in the hallway.

In a second, Flame's sense of satisfaction had disappeared. The Sprite Sisters looked round in horror.

'Where are we?' whispered Marina.

'How are we going to find the portal?' cried Ariel.

Flame's hands were clammy, her heart pounding. She did not know. How would they get back?

'What do we do now?' whispered Ash, her face white as a sheet.

Flame looked around her quickly. George had said he did not have long when he came to them in the tower, she thought. What if they were running out of time now?

Ash interrupted her thoughts. 'How do we get back?' she whispered.

Flame tensed with sudden realisation. 'Up!' she said. 'We must go up!' And she turned to run up the rickety wooden stairs. Her sisters followed close behind.

As they mounted the steps, the house got darker and darker.

'I don't like this!' squeaked Ariel.

'Come on, don't stop!' urged Marina, behind her.

At the top of the house, in almost complete darkness, Flame opened a door into an empty attic.

'In here, quick!' she cried.

The four sisters burst into the darkened room. Immediately, Flame grabbed Marina and Ariel's hand. 'Hold hands,' she said, as Ash grabbed hands too.

'We're running out of time,' whispered Marina. 'I can feel it!'

'We're going to be trapped,' whimpered Ariel.

'No we're not!' urged Flame. 'Quickly, quickly – make the Circle of Power!'

Meanwhile, on the driveway at Sprite Towers, Glenda Glass stood by her silver car, her hands clenched with rage. Once again, she had failed to get into the house. The battle with Mrs Duggery had been hard, but brief. The old lady with the lilac knitted hat was still the more powerful, and Glenda had retreated.

Now she stood under the dark, moonless sky and focused

her mind on the Sprite Sisters. Those girls are somewhere in the portal, she thought. I can feel it.

Well, they can stay there, she thought, a grim smile moving across her face. There's one more thing I can try . . .

She leaned back against the car and fixed the image of Margaret Sprite in her mind.

'Grandmother,' she called through time. 'Grandmother! Listen to me! Shut the door! Shut the door to the portal! Stop the Sprite Sisters coming back!'

Sitting in the high-backed chair by the fire, Margaret stared at the photograph of Sidney and herself, those two happy children – and she began to cry. Then, somewhere through her grief, she heard a voice calling. 'Grandmother!' the voice called. 'Grandmother!' she heard again. In the midst of her tears, the voice called again. 'Close the portal! Help me trap the Sprite Sisters in the portal!'

For a second, Margaret wavered. A sudden feeling swept over her, as she realised that her granddaughter was calling to her through time. For a second, the memory of dark magic flashed into her mind. I need to help her, she thought, tensing. She wants me to close the portal. The attic, she thought. The girls will leave through the attic.

'Stop the girls coming back!' the voice called again. Margaret moved forward in her seat to rise – then stopped. She stared again at the photograph between her fingers.

No, she thought, sitting back down. I will not use dark magic again. I have found what I was really looking for – love. I will honour the Sprite Code of Honour – it's what

Sidney always wanted.

And, as a sense of lightness and well-being passed over Margaret Sprite, her face softened. I have all I need, she thought. I have found what I was really looking for. It was there all the time, but I chose not to see it. I will not hurt Sidney's great-great-granddaughters.

And she called back to the voice in her mind. 'No, I will not help you. I will not use dark magic against those girls.'

As she settled further into the chair, she saw in her mind the four girls creating the rainbow of light in the attic room. Through the light appeared the small door of a portal.

They've found the door, she thought. But the light is already dimming – the girls have been too long here. The door is getting smaller. Soon it will be too small for them to pass through . . .

She saw the four girls stare at the shrinking door in horror. She saw the girl with the copper-coloured hair push her three sisters – the little blond one, the brown-haired girl and the dark-haired one – through the door, one by one, as fast as she could.

But the door was almost closed, and as the copper-haired girl flung herself through the now tiny space, Margaret saw it snap shut behind her, just missing the girl's feet.

Thank goodness, she thought. Thank goodness.

And, as Margaret's heart opened, Glenda Glass slumped against her car. Her jaw was clenched, her pride wounded, and anger filled her heart.

She did not help me, she thought. Margaret did not help me . . . Something has changed . . .

* * *

In the West Tower room of Sprite Towers, Charles Smythson stared in panic. In front of him the arc of white light and the rainbow of light were fading. Second by second, the steps to the portal were fading.

The portal is closing – and the girls are still in there, he thought, his heart pumping furiously. Oh my God – what can I *do*? What can I do to stop the door closing?

I've got to put something in the light to keep it open, he thought, frantically looking round the empty tower room. Keep it open, don't let it close!

What with? There was nothing in the room.

With a mounting sense of desperation, he looked down at his hands and arms.

My arm! I'll have to put my arm in, he thought. And he reached into the rainbow of light and felt it close around his arm.

The Sprite Sisters spun and whirled in the fast-fading rainbow.

'The light's going!' screamed Marina, her arms flailing.

'We're going to be trapped!' shouted Ariel, her body whooshing round and round.

'Grab my hand, Ariel!' screamed Ash, as her little sister sped past.

'The Circle of Power!' shouted Marina. 'We must make the Circle of Power and keep the portal open!'

'Flame!' cried Ash, seeing her older sister's exhausted, pale face drop on to her chest. 'Flame, wake up! We've got to make the Circle of Power!'

Marina, Ariel and Ash thrashed and flailed their way together, grabbing on to one another as hard as they could.

'Quick, grab Flame!' shouted Marina.

Suddenly, they were all connected, all holding hands as they spun through time.

'What's happening?' asked Flame, blearily.

'We're in the portal!' shouted Ash. 'Come on, Flame – wake up! We must hold the light!'

'Stay with us, Flame!' cried Ariel.

'Quickly, quickly – the Circle of Power! Flame, *come on*!' shouted Marina.

'*Please, Flame – wake up!*' cried Ariel.

Hearing her little sister's desperate cry, Flame stirred. 'The door!' she murmured. 'I can feel it closing.'

Then she murmured, 'Mrs Duggery.'

'*Mrs Duggery – help us!*' cried Ariel, Marina and Ash with all their might.

A moment later, seeing her eldest sister's head drop again, Marina cried, 'Come on, Flame – hold tight! We must make the Circle of Power!'

Their hands clutched tight to each other, the four sisters closed their eyes and summoned their magic power. In an instant, a bright blue light shone around their spinning bodies.

In the West Tower room, Charles Smythson felt his arm would break. The pressure around it was getting tighter and tighter and the pain was now so intense he thought he would scream.

'I can't stand it!' he cried, gritting his teeth. 'What do I do? What do I do? What do I do?'

Then, suddenly, someone was behind him. Charles gasped in astonishment.

An old lady – a very, very old lady with a lilac knitted hat and a face like a wrinkled walnut – touched his shoulder.

'Thas all right,' she said. 'I's here now. Took me a bit a time ter get up them stairs.'

'It's closing!' he cried. 'The portal is shrinking!'

''Ere, let me take tha from you,' she said, reaching over him and thrusting her tiny right arm into the rainbow light.

Charles yanked out his arm and fell back on to the floor. 'Blimey, that hurt!' he cried out, shaking his fingers.

For the next minute, he rubbed his arm as hard as he could, trying to get his blood flowing again. When he next looked round, the old lady with the lilac knitted hat was standing in the arc of light, her arm thrust out, her eyes glinting.

'The light's getting stronger!' exclaimed Charles, pulling himself up.

The old lady turned to give him a flinty smile. Around her arm, the rainbow of light brightened and widened.

A few seconds later, white light burst through the rainbow of light as steps appeared in the tower room.

Charles stared in amazement. The old woman kept her arm in the light. All the time, she was muttering, as if talking to someone.

Moment by moment, the light got stronger until it filled the room.

Charles held his breath and waited.

And then, on the steps, he saw a pair of feet appear. A moment later, the four Sprite Sisters staggered down the steps and fell on to the wooden floor.

CHAPTER EIGHTEEN

REVELATIONS AT SPRITE TOWERS

As the sun rose over Sprite Towers on Saturday morning, Mrs Duggery and Charles Smythson sat in the kitchen drinking coffee and eating chocolate biscuits.

Upstairs on the first floor, Mum and Dad slept on, oblivious of the night's activity.

On the second floor of the house, the four Sprite Sisters were sound asleep – still dressed in the clothes they had pulled on in the dark, in the early hours of the morning.

When the girls tumbled out of the portal, Charles Smythson had made his way down the back staircase to the kitchen. Mrs Duggery took the girls down the main staircase to their rooms on the floor below – without waking their parents. When they were all safely tucked in, albeit fully dressed, Mrs Duggery walked, very quietly, down the wide, mahogany staircase.

Charles was slumped in the Windsor chair by the Aga, fast asleep, when she entered the huge, stone-floored kitchen around three-thirty a.m. She put on the kettle to make some coffee and opened a packet of chocolate biscuits, and then she sat down and waited.

Around six-thirty a.m., Charles woke up and was startled to find the old woman with piercing eyes watching him across the big oak table. After a cup of coffee and some biscuits, he began to feel more alive. His arm was still sore and his head pounded.

There was much the two Sprites had to discuss. Charles had heard of Violet Duggery, of course – she was the oldest and most powerful of all the Sprites now living. But, up to this point, he had never met her. Now, he had a lot of questions to ask – the chief one being how to rid himself of Glenda Glass and the hold she had over him.

Mrs Duggery knew the strength of Glenda's power and will and she saw Charles needed some help. Marilyn Sprite had planted the seed in Charles's mind that he had a choice in the way he used his power. Now Mrs Duggery needed to help him get Glenda off his back, and keep her off his back. He'd been brave, she reasoned, and needed a chance to strengthen his good magic. So, in exchange for a promise that he would only henceforth use his power for good, Mrs Duggery taught Charles a way to create an impenetrable shield around himself.

'Yer earned it,' she said, tucking into another chocolate biscuit.

'Thank you,' he smiled.

* * *

When Dad pottered down in his dressing gown at half past seven, humming to himself, the last thing he expected to find was Charles Smythson and Mrs Duggery sitting in the kitchen.

'*Good Lord!*' he exclaimed, opening the door. 'Charles! Mrs Duggery!'

Charles stood up and walked towards Dad.

Dad's mouth dropped open like a fish.

'Morning, Colin,' said Charles, grabbing Dad's hand and shaking it. He gave Dad a warm smile. 'I hope you don't mind my coming so early. I had a rotten night – couldn't sleep, so decided to drive up to Sprite Towers. Miss the traffic and all that.'

Dad blinked in astonishment. 'It's nice to see you, but how . . . ?'

His voice trailed off, as Charles turned to Mrs Duggery at the table and said quickly, 'Mrs Duggery let me in.'

Dad stared at the tiny old lady in the lilac knitted hat.

She nodded at Charles. 'Thas right.'

'But how . . . ?' Dad waited for further explanation – but none was forthcoming.

Mrs Duggery started munching her umpteenth chocolate biscuit. Charles smiled politely and shrugged.

Dad put his hands in his pockets and bit his bottom lip.

'Mornin' Colin,' said Mrs Duggery, fixing him with her impenetrable stare.

Dad gulped, then said, politely, 'Good morning, Mrs Duggery.'

For a few seconds, he stood there, completely baffled. He shook his head. 'But I'm sure I locked the door . . .'

He looked at the table, registering the dirty mugs and the empty packets of chocolate biscuits. He looked at Mrs Duggery, noted her inscrutable face, and sighed.

Then, as if in answer to his unspoken question, she said, 'I were jus' passin'.'

'Right,' said Dad, in a tone that said, 'Well of course that explains everything.' Then he took a deep breath. Oh well, he thought, no harm's been done – and they are both family . . .

Archie was clawing at his pyjama trousers and Bert was yelping to be let out. Dad scratched his head again, then walked towards the back door and unlocked it.

The dogs careered out to the garden, barking away. Pudding trotted in and looked around disdainfully at the human beings.

'I'll just go and get dressed,' said Dad. 'I'd better tell Ottalie you're here.'

'Well, don't rush – we're fine,' said Charles.

Mum was equally surprised by the early morning visit, but greeted her visitors warmly and set to cooking a hearty breakfast.

'Where are the girls?' she asked Dad, as he walked into the kitchen holding the newspapers.

'Haven't seen them,' he replied.

'Odd – they're usually down by now.' Mum thought for a minute, wondering whether to cook more food for the girls or whether to wait.

Mrs Duggery answered the question she had been asking in her mind. 'Let 'em sleep,' she said, coming up beside Mum. 'They needs their rest – they's growin'.'

Mum smiled. 'Yes, you're right. I'll cook their breakfast when they come down.'

'Lovely smell,' said Charles. 'Boy, am I hungry! I could eat a horse this morning!'

'What, even after three packets of chocolate biscuits?' laughed Mum.

Charles grinned. 'That was – mostly – Mrs Duggery!'

Mrs Duggery smiled the smallest smile.

Fifteen minutes later, the breakfast was ready: crisp bacon, plump sausages, juicy mushrooms, fried eggs and a huge pile of toast.

Mum, Dad, Charles and Mrs Duggery sat down at the kitchen table and tucked in.

Dad poured glasses of apple juice, pressed from the fruit grown in their own orchard, while Charles poured cups of fresh coffee.

'So, tell us about the inventory, Charles,' said Mum. 'I'm dying to know how it all worked out.'

While Mum, Dad and Charles ate and nattered about the portraits at Sprite Towers, Mrs Duggery made her way through a huge plate of breakfast. She munched, silent but content.

The conversation rattled on. At ten o'clock, Mum realised that none of her daughters had yet appeared for breakfast.

'It's not like them to sleep this late,' she said, looking up at the big, old-fashioned clock high on the wall. 'I'd better go and see if they're okay.'

Mrs Duggery stood up. 'Tha's awright, my dear,' she said. 'You sit her' an' enjoy yer chat with Charles. I'll go an' get 'em up.'

'Oh – okay,' said Mum, surprised. 'Thank you.'

Dad smiled across at her. Mum shrugged and sat back down again. There was no arguing with Mrs Duggery.

She is so strange, thought Mum, watching the old lady stomp out of the kitchen in her big brown boots. Dad grinned, knowing what she was thinking.

Charles gulped, aware that, now they were alone, Dad might ask him how Mrs Duggery let him in. He was saved by Marilyn Sprite's arrival.

'Hello!' she called from the hallway. 'I'm home!'

'Ma!' said Dad, getting up. He walked through to the hallway, smiling, and gave his mother a big hug. 'Good to see you! Did you have a good trip?'

As she came into the kitchen, Marilyn Sprite gave Charles Smythson a tepid smile. After his last visit to Sprite Towers, she was not yet sure if he was in the house as friend or foe.

Charles smiled at her warmly, trying to reassure her with his gaze. When she asked where the girls were, he said quickly, 'Mrs Duggery's upstairs waking them.'

'Mrs Duggery?' Grandma looked startled. If Mrs Duggery was here, it must mean her granddaughters had been up to magic, she thought – probably with their visit to the portal. She glanced at Charles, in acknowledgement, collected herself and said nothing.

Charles smiled a quick smile, which seemed to say, 'They're safe and all is well.'

'Charles got here at the crack of dawn,' interjected Dad, pouring his mother some coffee.

'Really?' Marilyn looked at Charles – and smiled.

'Found him and Mrs Duggery in the kitchen when I came down to let out the animals,' added Dad. 'Gave me quite a shock.'

Grandma laughed. 'Well, you've had worse, love!'

'Yes, life at Sprite Towers is full of surprises,' replied Dad, sitting down again.

'What's happened to the ghost?' asked Grandma.

'I haven't seen it since the party,' said Mum. She looked around, a puzzled look on her face. Then she said, 'It feels much nicer in here today. I wonder if it's gone?'

'It does feel brighter and warmer,' said Dad. 'Something's changed.' He turned to Charles. 'Did you know we had a ghost here?'

'Good heavens!' said Charles.

'Let's hope that dratted ghost has finally left then,' said Mum. 'It gave me the shivers.'

Grandma looked round and caught Charles's glance. He knows what's happened, she thought.

Mum and Dad were itching to ask Grandma if she'd had any success with her fraud investigations. But, unaware that Charles already knew of Marilyn's suspicions about Glenda Glass, they hesitated to bring up the subject.

Instead, Dad launched into stories about the ghost and the Hallowe'en party, and for the next half-hour the conversation bowled along.

Upstairs, the Sprite Sisters were dog-tired. Flame, particularly, felt as if she'd been hit on the head. It had taken Mrs

Duggery several minutes to wake her fully.

As quickly as possible, the tiny old lady in the lilac knitted hat got the girls up, showered and into fresh clothes. The clothes they'd slept in were either tucked away into drawers or smuggled into the washing basket.

Before they all went down, Mrs Duggery told them they needed to go first to the West Tower room. Blearily, they followed her up the stairs, along the attics corridor and up the rickety stairs. The round tower room looked friendly and warm in the autumn light. The sky shone blue behind the high, glass dome.

'Do you remember what happened?' asked Mrs Duggery, standing in the middle of the room.

The Sprite Sisters leaned sleepily against the wall. Flame started to say something – then went quiet again. Ariel stared into space. Marina shook her head.

'It's all a bit hazy,' said Ash.

They looked at Mrs Duggery. 'What happened?'

'Yer went in ter the portal, thas what happened,' she said, her black eyes glinting.

'Oh yes,' said Marina, rubbing her eyes. 'I remember now . . . '

Mrs Duggery looked around at them. 'Well dun, all a' you. That were quite a trip yer made las' night.'

Flame frowned. 'I remember pushing my sisters into the portal – then it all went blank.'

'Well, George were right when he tol' you tha' there's only a little time when yer come through a portal,' explained Mrs Duggery. 'An you were a while with Margaret – longer than wha' yer realised. So the power, tha' weren't ser strong, when yer came home. Yer lucky yer got back at all – all a' you.' She looked at Flame, then said, 'Yer dun yer sisters proud, Flame. You was very brave.'

Flame smiled at the old lady in the lilac knitted hat. 'Thank you,' she said quietly.

Mrs Duggery looked around at Marina, Ash and Ariel. 'You wer all brave.'

'I remember spinning and whirling,' said Marina.

'I remember us all shouting and crying,' added Ash.

'I remember us calling you,' said Ariel.

Mrs Duggery nodded. 'I 'erd yer.'

'So what happened here, in the tower room?' asked Flame.

'Well, lucky for yer, Charles Smythson were 'ere already.'

'*Charles?*' asked Flame, astonished.

'Yes, Charles,' said Mrs Duggery. 'Yer got a lot ter thank him fer.'

The girls exchanged amazed glances.

Mrs Duggery crossed her tiny arms over her tiny chest and explained. 'He drove up las' night in a panic – reckoned summat were about ter happen ter yer. An' that *did*: the portal nearly closed on yer. Yer wouldn't hav' bin able ter get out if that'd closed – so Charles stuck his arm in and held it open. Good thing he were ser brave, otherwise yer'd a bin stuck out there for ever.'

Mrs Duggery was silent for a few seconds, then she said, 'Don't yer remember seein' Charles as yer fell out a the portal?'

The Sprite Sisters shook their heads.

'Oh, well, he were 'ere – and he helped yer. Yer need ter thank him.'

Flame looked the tiny old lady in the eye. 'We will. And thank you for telling us.'

Marina yawned, then asked, 'When did you arrive, Mrs Duggery?'

'Well, I come ter stop Glenda Glass gettin' in the house las' night. Reckon she'd a' closed the portal, too, if she'd got up 'ere. But I put a stop ter her. By the time I got up ter the tower, Charles's arm had nearly fallen off.'

She looked around at the Sprite Sisters, her eyes glinting.

The Sprite Sisters blinked in amazement.

'So what did you do?' asked Ariel.

'Opened up the portal an' got yer all hum.'

The Sprite Sisters sighed heavily. 'Thank you,' they said.

'Thas awright,' said Mrs Duggery, with a small smile.

'So what happened to Margaret?' asked Marina, looking around the tower. 'Is she still here?'

Mrs Duggery shook her head. 'She's gorn.'

'Will she come back?' asked Ariel.

'No, she's got wha' she really needed,' said Mrs Duggery. She turned to Flame and said, 'Tha' were a good idea with the photograph. Tha' opened Margaret's heart agin. That'd bin dead a long, long time. You found a way ter heal her and yer did well ter think on it.'

'Thank you,' said Flame, humbled by this praise.

'What about Glenda?' asked Ash.

Mrs Duggery gave a short, sharp laugh. 'My Lord, tha' woman is incredible!'

'How do you mean?' asked Ash.

Mrs Duggery shook her head. 'Well, she just don't never

give up, do she? Margaret won't hurt yer no more, but yer'll still have Glenda Glass ter del with.'

The Sprite Sisters looked at one another with glum faces.

'There's summat else I got ter tell yer.'

The Sprite Sisters waited.

'Yer got ter take care of Verena. She's goin' ter need sum help.'

'How?' asked Flame.

Mrs Duggery shook her head. 'All I'm sayin' is look after her. The time's coming when she'll need some help from you girls. Tha' won't be easy fer her.'

The Sprite Sisters exchanged glances.

'An' there's another thing,' added Mrs Duggery. 'Your power – tha's gettin' stronger. I want yer all ter promise that you'll take good care on it. I want yer ter promise me yer'll only ever use it fer good.'

'But of course,' said Flame, slightly offended. 'Why do you think we might misuse it?'

Mrs Duggery looked the eldest Sprite in the eye. 'Flame, thas easy ter get tempted when yer got a magic power. There's things out there you int never dreamed of. You'll meet 'em as you get older and yer power gets stronger. So you jus' take care and remember what I told yer.'

Flame drew a sharp breath. 'Then thank you for warning us,' she said, quietly.

Mrs Duggery looked around at them all. 'Now, do you promise to only use yer magic power for good?'

The four Sprite Sisters nodded. 'Yes, we promise,' they said. They waited, silent, as Mrs Duggery stood there thinking.

What might she say next, they wondered. But suddenly, the tiny old lady moved to the door and said, 'Now come yer on down, otherwise yer mother'll be wonderin' was goin' on. Yer grandma's back, too.'

'Hang on – what will we say to Mum and Dad?' asked Flame. 'Mum is sure to ask why we're up so late.'

Mrs Duggery turned, gave Flame a flinty smile. 'That yer all a bit tired after a busy week.'

Flame nodded. 'Yes, you're right.' She smiled at Mrs Duggery. 'Thank you so much for all your help.'

Mrs Duggery nodded. 'You're very welcome, my dear. Now, get yers downstairs and have some breakfast. Yer grandma's lookin' forward ter seein' yer all.'

'Morning, girls!' said Dad, as the Sprite Sisters walked into the kitchen, followed by Mrs Duggery.

Mum jumped up. 'Goodness, you all look tired! Let me get you some breakfast.'

'It's lovely to see you, girls,' said Grandma, giving each of them a big hug.

'We've missed you,' said Flame.

'Hello, girls!' said Charles, waving from the table.

As she watched her granddaughters smiling back at him, Marilyn Sprite noticed that they were all much warmer towards Charles than on his last visit. She looked at Mrs Duggery, who responded with a small nod. The gesture was enough to make Marilyn realise that Charles had played some part in whatever had happened last night.

A few minutes later, Mum put plates of hot food down in

front of the girls and they all tucked in.

'I'm starving!' said Flame, through a mouthful of egg.

'Me, too,' said Marina, grabbing a third sausage.

Mum laughed. 'Why is everyone so hungry today?'

The Sprite Sisters grinned. 'This is heaven!' squeaked Ariel, through a mouthful of fried bread.

'Whatever have you all been doing, to make you sleep so late and give you this appetite?' asked Mum.

'Growing!' said Ash, buttering another piece of toast. 'We're *growing* girls!'

Everyone laughed. Even Mrs Duggery smiled.

'Can we go and have a look at this new borehole of yours?' Charles asked Dad.

'Wait till we've finished!' cried Ariel. 'We'll come out with you.'

'Of course, Charles,' said Dad. 'Okay, okay – you lot finish your breakfast.'

'Brunch,' corrected Mum. 'We've been here for hours.'

Dad grinned, then turned to Mrs Duggery. 'Violet, I wonder if you know the layout of the old house under the lawn? If so, it would be interesting if you'd show us.'

Mrs Duggery gave a sharp nod. 'Righty-ho,' she said.

Dad smiled to himself. She must be over a hundred if she knows that, he thought.

Meanwhile, Archie was trying to eat the lace on Charles's shoe. 'Archie, stop it!' he said, pushing the puppy gently away.

'Archie will be chewing the furniture next,' said Dad.

'A puppy was your idea,' said Mum, giving him a 'look'.

'Labradors chew everything,' said Flame. 'I've been reading

about them. Sometimes vets find their stomachs full of stones they've eaten.'

'We'll come down one morning and Archie will have eaten all the furniture!' exclaimed Ariel. 'There'll be nothing left.'

'Perhaps we should leave him in Dad's office for a few days – that'd soon clear things up,' suggested Flame, grinning.

'Ha, ha, ha,' retorted Dad.

Soon after, they all put on their coats and wellies and went out to the garden. Mrs Duggery stomped about in her big brown boots and showed them where the old house had been. First of all she walked the length of it, then the breadth. Then she showed them where the individual rooms had been.

'This 'ere were the drawin' room,' she said, waving her tiny arms. 'The fireplace – tha' were right 'ere. That were an inglenook – right big fire, tha' were.'

'What about the cellar?' asked Flame. 'Where was that?'

Mrs Duggery stopped, clamping a tiny hand around her chin. 'Well, now, let me think a moment . . .'

She marched towards the borehole. 'That were under 'ere,' she said, pointing. She lifted the lid of the shaft and peered in. 'This 'ere is where the ghost came up,' she said, in a matter-of-fact voice.

'Well, thank goodness we won't be drilling any more bore-holes,' laughed Dad. 'Goodness know what else we'd find here!'

Mrs Duggery fixed him with her glinting eyes. 'You might laugh, Colin, but thar's a lot a' things that happen right under people's noses – and they never knows.'

Dad gulped. 'I'm sure you're right.'

While Charles and Dad looked at the pump, the Sprite Sisters stood with Mrs Duggery a little way off.

'I'll be orf now,' said Mrs Duggery. 'Now, 'fore I go there's summat else yer all ought ter know.'

'What?' the sisters asked, wide-eyed.

'Thare's treasure here,' said the old lady, with a mysterious smile.

'What sort of treasure?' asked Ash.

'Look at George's plan. See where tha' guides you. And don't forget what I said about Verena.'

Just then, Grandma came over the lawn towards them. 'Violet,' she smiled. 'I expect you'll be off soon – but I'd love to have a chat.'

'Course,' said Mrs Duggery with her warmest smile. She had a soft spot for Marilyn Sprite.

'Let's go and sit in the library,' said Grandma.

And the two women walked into the house.

Flame, Marina, Ash and Ariel stood together, feeling more awake now with the cool autumn air on their faces.

'What now?' asked Ash, turning to look at Dad and Charles.

Dad beckoned them over. 'Bonfire!' he called.

The girls smiled and walked over to him.

'Bonfire?' said Charles.

'For the fireworks party tomorrow,' said Dad. 'Stephen and Verena will be coming. Do hope you'll stay for it.'

Charles smiled. 'I'd be delighted. I'll give you a hand now – got to pop over and see Stephen after lunch.'

'Okey-doke,' said Dad.

They all set about completing the huge bonfire they had begun the previous Saturday at the edge of the Big Field. Charles drove the small, ride-on tractor that served also as Dad's lawnmower. Towing the trailer, he carted some old bits of furniture that Mum thought were not worth saving, from the stables to the Big Field. Then they all went to the Wild Woods and filled a trailer there.

The Sprites had a late lunch of homemade vegetable soup and bread that day. Mrs Duggery agreed to stay and they all sat together around the big kitchen table. Underneath, Archie tried to chew Charles's shoelaces again, and there was more hilarity.

Afterwards, the Sprite Sisters followed Mrs Duggery outside to her huge boneshaker bicycle, propped against the wall.

'I wish you would stay with us,' said Ariel.

Mrs Duggery smiled. 'Thas very nice a yer, Ariel, but I hev ter git home.'

'Where is "home"?' asked Ariel. 'Is it far away?'

Mrs Duggery smiled again, but gave no answer.

Ariel looked at her sisters: they all shrugged. They had never got an answer from Mrs Duggery on this subject. Where Mrs Duggery went to, when she cycled off down the drive, was a mystery.

'Still, I wish you wouldn't go,' Ariel said again.

Mrs Duggery held out her tiny hand. On the top was a red ladybird with black spots. 'Here, take this,' she said and passed it to Ariel. The small blond-haired girl watched the insect on the back of her hand and she smiled at Mrs Duggery.

'Thas a Bishy Barney Bee,' said Mrs Duggery. 'When yer see him, yer'll know I'm around.'

'Why will seeing one make me think of you?' asked Ariel.

'Cause that just will,' said Mrs Duggery.

'Bishy Barney Bee . . . I like that name,' said Ariel. 'Thank you.' And she gave the old lady in the lilac knitted hat a big smile.

Mrs Duggery looked at the girls. 'Well, my dears, do you take care now,' she said.

Flame came towards her and gave her a brief hug. 'Thank you for everything,' she said.

When Marina, Ash and Ariel had said their thanks and goodbyes, Mrs Duggery climbed on to her bicycle. It seemed much bigger than her. With her tiny legs going like very slow pistons, she cycled off down the long drive.

The Sprite Sisters watched her.

'I wish she wouldn't go,' said Ariel.

'She makes me laugh,' grinned Marina.

'Thank goodness she came to our rescue last night,' said Flame.

'Yes,' agreed Ash. 'We must thank Charles – as she said.'

CHAPTER NINETEEN

REVELATIONS AT THE OAKS

A LITTLE while later, Charles knocked on the front door of The Oaks.

As he waited, he reminded himself that he had invoked new, magical protection – Mrs Duggery's shield – and that he was safe from Glenda Glass.

'Come in, Charles,' she said, opening the door.

He walked into the spacious hall.

'Coffee?'

'Thank you.' He followed her through to the kitchen.

'I thought Stephen might be here by now,' said Charles, looking round the huge, modern room. It's a very different kitchen from Sprite Towers, he thought. You can see the money in this house.

'He'll be here shortly,' said Glenda, pouring boiling water into the coffee pot.

Charles carried the coffee tray through to the drawing room and they sat down.

'Where's Verena? I was looking forward to meeting her.'

'She's been upstairs for hours. I expect she's talking to her friends on the phone,' replied Glenda, pouring out the coffee. 'So,' she said, handing him a cup and sitting down. 'What have you got to tell me?'

'I hear you met with Mrs Duggery.'

Glenda smiled a thin smile. 'You were at Sprite Towers before me.'

'Yes,' he nodded.

'And you found the conservatory door open?'

'Yes.'

Glenda smiled another thin smile. 'It was closed when I tried it – but I believe Mrs Duggery had something to do with that.'

'Thank heavens,' said Charles, softly.

'Why "thank heavens"?'

The expression on Charles's face hardened. 'We're very lucky those girls came back in one piece, Glenda. You should be ashamed of yourself in trying to hurt them! You and that grandmother of yours!'

Glenda raised an eyebrow. 'And how is Margaret? She's gone strangely quiet on me.'

'It seems Flame Sprite found a way to heal Margaret's anger. The ghost has left the house. Perhaps Margaret no longer wishes to communicate with you.'

'Rubbish!'

'Oh, for goodness sake give it up, Glenda!' said Charles, exasperated. 'Stop stirring up all this enmity and hatred!' He stood up, walked towards the window and gazed out over the lawn, sighing heavily. 'I've given the matter of our spy/paymaster relationship a lot of thought over the last few months. I've decided I do not wish to continue it.'

'You haven't been hasty to say no to the money I paid you previously,' retorted Glenda, acidly.

'The price is too high,' said Charles, turning towards her, his face reddening. 'I want no further part of this. I don't share your hatred of the Sprite family. In fact, I'm very fond of them. And they are that: *family.*'

'Tell me what Marilyn has found out in France,' Glenda cut in.

Charles gave a small laugh. 'I have no idea – she hasn't told me! She was looking after a sick friend, as far as I know.'

Glenda sipped her coffee, her face impassive.

Charles turned – realised, suddenly, how angry this woman made him. Outrage boiled up in him, as he looked at her.

'You are a despicable human being. You use your magic power to hurt and harm, without any regard to the consequences – as if it's something to play with! You *know* what happens when we Sprites misuse our magic power! You *know* the harm it causes! *Why* do you do it? Why can't you see that it isolates you! You sit here in this house – you have no friends. Nobody likes you. Verena is miserable living with you. You dare not trust anyone. And you really want to live like that?'

228

Glenda stood up and walked towards Charles. 'Who told you that Verena is miserable?' she demanded, standing directly in front of him.

'The Sprites, of course! The whole family knows. Even Stephen knows.'

Charles looked Glenda straight in the eye. Then he said more quietly, 'If Verena knew you'd deliberately broken up her parents' marriage, she would never forgive you.'

Glenda raised an eyebrow. 'How do you know I did?'

'A few things you have said, and I know you well enough to know how you organise things. Zoe would never have left without being pushed!'

Glenda turned away and sat down on the sofa.

'Glenda, you have *got* to stop using your power to hurt people!' continued Charles, his voice intense. 'You have to let people lead the lives they want to lead. You've stolen Marilyn's money. You've wrecked your son's marriage and alienated your grandchild. You're jealous of the Sprite Sisters and Marilyn. You've tried several times to hurt them – and to destroy Sprite Towers. For heaven's sake, just let everyone be! Return Marilyn's money and go back to the south of France. Take your scheming and your jealousy away from here. Nobody is safe around you.'

Glenda watched him, her eyes cold as ice.

'And let *me* be, Glenda,' said Charles, softly. 'Let me be – because I am not doing any more dirty work for you. Never again.'

As he said this, Glenda lifted her hand and sent out a bolt of power. She expected it to hit him in the chest, but instead of reeling sideways he stood still.

Glenda stared at him, surprised.

Charles's voice was cold, deliberate. 'You can't hurt me any more.'

Glenda gave a harsh laugh. 'Has that old crone helped you to strengthen your magic?'

'If you mean Mrs Duggery, then yes, she has. And I've promised her I will never again misuse my magic. That's a hard thing to do, when you know the power it can give you. But I shall honour my promise to strengthen my good magic. So, no more, Glenda. No more.'

Glenda stood silent. The tension crackled in the air.

Then Charles said, 'Where is it?'

Glenda turned. 'Where is what?'

'Marilyn's money.'

Glenda snorted. 'Grow up, Charles! You really expect me to tell you that?'

Outside on the drive there was a scrunch of gravel. Glenda looked round. 'Stephen is here,' she said, coolly. And she walked out of the drawing room to open the front door.

A moment later, Charles heard her say, 'Stephen, darling!' and noted the warmth in her voice. He gazed out of the window at the trees across the lawn. Then a girl's voice exclaimed, 'Daddy!' and Stephen and Verena came into the room.

'Charles! Great to see you, old chap!' said Stephen, shaking his hand warmly. He turned to Verena, 'I don't believe you've met my daughter.'

'Hello Verena. I've heard a lot about you,' said Charles,

smiling as he shook her hand.

'And I've heard a lot about you,' she said, colouring slightly.

'It's amazing we've never met before,' said Charles.

He glanced at Glenda. She looked happy – like a normal grandmother with her family. She's unbelievable, he thought. Look at her now – no one would ever guess her real character. For a second, Charles felt astonished, appalled, outraged at the conversation they'd had only minutes before. He glanced at Verena. There's something about her. It's as if she is wearing a mask . . . And he realised that his young cousin was watching him with an intense gaze – a gaze of curiosity.

For the next hour, they all sat in the drawing room and chatted. Stephen and Charles talked about the inventory at Sprite Towers and new work: Stephen had another client lined up for his cousin. Charles thanked him warmly.

Glenda sat, smiling, as if this was a normal Saturday afternoon, as if nothing untoward had been said between her and Charles. Verena looked happy and listened politely.

Then Charles made his farewell. Stephen saw him to the door and Charles thanked him again.

'Will we see you tomorrow evening at the fireworks?' asked Stephen.

'Yes,' smiled Charles.

'Excellent,' said Stephen.

Having waited to see her father for so long, Verena was bursting to talk to him. 'Let's go for a walk, Daddy! I want to talk with you.'

Stephen smiled at her, looked round at his mother. Glenda

shrugged. 'You go, dear. It's a nice afternoon.'

A short while after, Stephen and Verena set off through the woods. For the next hour and a half, they walked with their arms linked, smiling at each other happily. He told her about his trip to Japan. She told him about school and the Sprite's Hallowe'en party.

Then Stephen said, 'Ottalie and Colin called me. They've been worried that you're not happy living here with your grandmother.'

Verena nodded, silent.

'What's been happening?' asked Stephen.

Verena wanted to burst – then she stopped and said quietly, 'Grandma's different when you're not here. She's so cold.'

'Is she?'

'She's like ice, Daddy. She doesn't speak. She never hugs me. She's not interested in what I'm doing. She seems to hate the Sprites – and they don't like her. When she takes me over there, like to the party last week, she doesn't go in – and they don't invite her to.' Verena looked at her father. 'Mr and Mrs Sprite are lovely people. It's Grandma that's odd. She's not a nice person.'

Stephen stared ahead – and nodded. 'I thought she had changed. She was never much of a mother to me, when I was a boy. Then, when I grew up, I didn't see her for a long time – never met two of her husbands. But when your mother left, I needed her help – and she seemed so pleased to come and live here with you. I was delighted to see her again, after all those years. I was hoping we could make up for the lost time – and that she'd be a real grandmother to you.'

'She hasn't been,' said Verena, quietly.

Stephen shook his head. 'I realise that now – and I'm so sorry.'

'I'd rather have Mummy here. Do you think she will come back?'

Stephen smiled. 'I have spoken with her and I hope she will.'

'When?'

'Soon,' he said. 'I'll go out to Buenos Aires and bring her back.'

Verena burst into tears. 'I'm so pleased, Daddy!'

He grabbed her hand. 'So am I, sweetheart. So am I.'

They walked along happily. There was something else that Verena wanted to tell him – but she said nothing. For the moment, she put it to the back of her mind and enjoyed the time with her father.

But that night, as she lay in her bed, Verena thought about the conversation she had overheard that afternoon.

Glenda had told Charles Smythson that her granddaughter was upstairs on the phone. Neither of them had heard her move, silently, to the hall. Neither of them knew that Verena had listened to most of their argument.

Now there were so many questions. What did Grandma and Charles mean by 'magic'? What money had Grandma stolen from Marilyn Sprite? Why was she jealous of her and the Sprite Sisters? How did she try to destroy the house? Why was Charles shouting? What did he mean when he said Grandma couldn't hurt him any more? Why did they keep using the word 'power'? What was the 'power'?

Verena's mind whirred and whirred. So many questions –

but who to ask? Charles? Would he answer them?

As she lay there in the dark, Flame Sprite's face came into her mind. She pictured them standing in the corridor, at the Hallowe'en party. She remembered catching Flame's eye, as the ghost whirled around her. And she remembered her feeling of not being frightened – of just feeling curious.

Most of all, she remembered the strange and new sensation that she and Flame Sprite shared something – something that they had to keep secret.

I wish I could talk to Flame about it, she thought. If I did, I feel sure she would tell me, as she's so direct. But I don't think she trusts me. Perhaps she knows Grandma asks me to tell her things about the Sprites.

If I want to really talk to Flame, I have to let her know she can trust me. How can I win her trust?

CHAPTER TWENTY

FIREWORKS AT SPRITE TOWERS

ON SUNDAY morning, the Sprite Sisters, Charles and Dad put the finishing touches to the bonfire and set up the pots for the fireworks on the Big Field.

The bonfire was five metres high. 'I think that'll do,' said Dad, standing back to admire it.

'It looks good,' said Charles. 'Should be quite a blaze.'

'Especially if this wind keeps up,' agreed Dad.

Charles drove the ride-on tractor and trailer back to the stables. Flame, Marina and Ariel ran ahead to clean out the rabbit and guinea pig hutches. Ash walked with Dad.

'I like autumn,' said Ash, looking up at the trees. 'I love the colours and the dank smell and the frosty mornings.'

'Me, too,' agreed Dad.

'Two parties in one week is cool,' said Ash.

'Yes, you're lucky girls,' said Dad.

'We know,' said Ash, taking his hand.

He smiled down at her. 'I know you know.'

At lunchtime, they all sat down for roast beef, Yorkshire puddings and homegrown vegetables.

'My favourite lunch,' said Dad, as he carved the joint.

'What a fortnight!' said Mum, pushing back her wavy blond hair and sitting down.

'I'm glad the ghost has gone,' piped up Ariel.

Mum looked at Dad, then at Ariel. 'How do you know it's gone?' she asked.

Ariel was busy helping herself to some roast potatoes. 'Sidney told me.'

Mum looked at Charles and giggled. 'You must think we're all completely barking, Charles.'

'Only a little,' he smiled. He caught Ariel's eye and smiled at her. Ariel giggled, too.

'That's what Verena said the other day – that we were only partly bonkers,' said Dad.

'Oh Dad, you are sweet,' said Flame. 'You don't even know the half of it.'

He looked round at his eldest daughter. 'Well, perhaps one day you will explain.'

Flame nodded. 'Maybe,' she said.

Then Mum said, her voice slightly taut, 'Well, whatever all that ghost stuff was, I'm just glad it's over and done with.'

'I wonder why it just upped and left?' said Dad. 'Assuming Sidney is right, of course.'

'Of course Sidney is right, Dad – Sidney is always right!' said Ariel, with a look of exasperation.

'Then why don't you get him to help you with your maths homework?' asked Dad, with a twinkle in his eye.

'I hadn't thought of that!' giggled Ariel.

'Why does Sidney think the ghost has gone?' persisted Dad, as he tucked in.

'He said she was happy now, so she could go home.'

Dad made a face. 'Well, that's a relief.'

'Honestly, what nonsense,' muttered Mum.

The Sprite Sisters, Grandma and Charles exchanged glances and laughed quietly.

Then Grandma said, 'Ottalie, what time have you invited the others over?'

'Half past four,' replied Mum. 'I invited Harry and Charlotte and the children as well.'

'Good idea,' said Dad.

Mum frowned slightly. 'But I didn't invite Glenda.'

Everyone was silent as they thought on this. Then Charles said, 'She doesn't like parties.'

'Just as well, then,' smiled Mum.

After lunch, the grown-ups sat in the library by the fire. The girls, still tired from their late night, decided to watch a film in the snug and took Archie in as well.

As soon as they were alone, they started chattering about the ghost and Mum's reaction.

'Why didn't you tell us what Sidney said?' Flame asked Ariel.

'I only found out just before lunch,' said Ariel. 'And we already knew – as Mrs Duggery told us, yesterday. I was really telling Mum and Dad.'

'Good thinking,' said Flame.

'If Sidney's happy about Margaret, it must mean the plan's safe,' said Ash. She took out her magic stone from her pocket and looked at it.

'The plan is back in its box and Mrs Duggery told me it is safe there,' said Flame.

'That was quite a trip in the portal,' said Marina. 'Lucky that Charles and Mrs Duggery came to help us, or we might have been lost somewhere in time and space.'

Flame shuddered at this thought. She snuggled down into her chair. 'We must thank Charles before he goes.'

'Come on, let's watch this film,' said Ariel, burrowing into the corner of the sofa. Then she sat up again. 'Oh, yes, and one more thing – Sidney said to say thank you for helping Margaret.'

'That's good,' said Flame. 'I'm relieved we found a way to help her, as well as stop her.' And she switched on the film.

At four-thirty p.m., Stephen and Verena arrived, along with Harry and Charlotte and their children.

Mum and Grandma packed up hot sausages, bread rolls and baked potatoes in tin foil. Dad got out cans of cider for the grown-ups and fizzy drinks for the children. Charles was in charge of the box of fireworks. Stephen and Harry added the fireworks they'd brought – and they found they'd got quite a pile.

'Should be a cracking good display,' said Stephen.

Dad shut the dogs and Pudding in the kitchen. Then, all dressed up warm, they carried everything out to the bonfire on the Big Field.

It was a dark, windy night. As soon as Charles held the match to the fire, it blazed. Quickly, the flames leaped high. Everybody gasped and stepped back.

Mum, Grandma and Charlotte set out the food and drink on a trestle table that Charles had brought out on the trailer, and everyone tucked in.

For the first hour, they chatted and watched the fire, had a drink and ate their food. The children lit sparklers and made patterns against the firelight.

Flame stood next to Charles. 'Thank you so much for helping us the other night,' she said. 'We would have been lost without you.'

He smiled at her warmly. 'It was a close thing. Thank goodness Mrs Duggery turned up and stopped Glenda getting in.'

'You were very brave to put your arm into the portal to keep it open,' said Flame.

Charles nodded. 'So were you!'

'Well, thank you, anyway.'

'You're welcome, Flame – and I'm delighted you found a way to help Margaret. It was an intelligent way, you thought of, to solve the problem.' He stared into the fire. 'I just wish we could do the same for Glenda,' he said, quietly.

'You mean *help* her?' asked Flame, with a frown.

'Well, you healed Margaret's pain and stopped her trying to hurt you. Why shouldn't you do the same with Glenda?'

Flame looked at Charles with a thoughtful gaze. 'Hm – I shall think on that.'

They stared at the bonfire, silent, for a while. Then Flame turned and said, 'I'm glad we can trust you, Charles – that you're on our side.'

'Me, too.'

'What did Glenda say when you went round?' asked Flame.

'She wasn't pleased, as you'd expect. Apart from being angry that she hasn't got her hands on the plan, I think she may be rattled that your grandmother might be on to her about the money.'

'Really?'

'Really.'

'Have you told Grandma?'

'Yes,' replied Charles. 'But she knows Glenda will never admit she'd got the money or done anything wrong. Glenda is a smart, tough lady.'

Flame gave a wry smile. 'Don't we know it!'

Stephen came up and the two men started talking. Flame moved slightly apart and watched the fire.

Then Verena was beside her. 'Flame, there's something I want to ask you in private. Can we move over here a little way?'

'Okay,' said Flame, wondering what was coming, as they stepped back from the fire. Was this something about Quinn? And she braced herself for one of Verena's put-downs.

Verena's face was tense. Flame waited, aware suddenly of the girl's anxiety.

Verena looked down at her gloved hands, took a deep breath and launched in. 'Flame, please – I really need your help.'

'Okay.'

'What I'm about to say – you may think it's all nonsense. I honestly don't know what you will think – maybe that I'm stupid.'

Flame smiled softly. 'I'd never think you were stupid, Verena.'

Verena's face relaxed. 'Okay then. When Charles came over to The Oaks yesterday, I overheard him and Grandma talking.'

'Did they know you were listening?'

Verena shook her head. 'I know it's not good to listen to other people's conversations, but there are so many things about my grandmother that I don't understand.'

'Such as?'

'Such as why she's obsessed with you girls and Sprite Towers.'

Flame frowned. 'Oh,' she said, quietly.

'So I listened in,' said Verena. 'They were . . . they were talking about "power" and "magic". Charles got very cross with Grandma and said she had to stop hurting you and your sisters – to leave you alone. And he told her to give back your grandmother's money.'

Flame blinked, amazed. What would Verena say next? What did she know? Her heart began to beat faster.

'I know there's something happening that I don't know about,' continued Verena. 'I just . . . I just . . . *sense* that you might know what they're talking about. And I wondered . . . I wondered if you would explain?'

Flame stared at the fire. She could feel the intensity of Verena's gaze. She would have to say something – but what? The Sprites never discussed their magic power, but she found it impossible to lie. She turned and looked at Verena. 'Why don't you ask your grandmother?'

Verena looked imploringly at Flame. 'I know there's something, otherwise you wouldn't look so shocked. I don't want to hear whatever it is from my grandmother: I don't trust her.'

Flame nodded, silent.

'When I got back from the party the other night, Grandma wanted to know what happened with the ghost,' continued Verena. 'She's always asking me questions about you all. I told her I'd heard the ghost saying something to me in the corridor – you know, when you were watching. I know you saw it, too.'

Their eyes met.

'I told her the ghost had said the words, "magic power".'

Verena noticed Flame's eyes widen.

'What did your grandmother say to that?'

'She said . . . she said, "You'll find out when the time comes." That's what she said.'

Flame held Verena's gaze. 'Then you must wait.'

'Oh come on, *please*, Flame! I need to know! Tell me what this is about!'

Flame turned away. I can't lie, she thought, her mind

racing. I can't lie, but nor can I tell Verena . . .

For a minute, she stared at the fire, her mind spinning with conflicting emotions. Here was the girl who was Glenda Glass's spy. Here was her distant Sprite cousin. How had she heard the ghost? Did it mean that she, too, had got the magic power that ran through the family? Was this what her question was *really* about?

Flame thought back to her ninth birthday, when she had first felt the tingling in her fingers. If Grandma hadn't been there to tell me it was my magic power, what would I have done, she wondered. Who would I have asked?

But Verena hasn't got her power, she thought. If she had, she would have said something about a feeling in her hands – and she hasn't. Is she bluffing? No, I don't think so.

Verena waited.

Then Flame turned back and saw the girl's beseeching eyes. She smiled a kind smile. 'Listen, Verena, I'm sorry, I cannot tell you, but I promise that when you understand what the ghost meant, then I will talk to you about it.'

Verena gave a short, sharp laugh. 'But how will I understand what the ghost meant if you don't tell me?'

Flame looked at her intensely. 'You just will. Trust me.'

Verena shook her head. Her face looked sad, confused.

'You're not alone,' said Flame, putting her hands on Verena's arm. 'I know you feel it right now – but you're not. And one day, you may understand why I cannot tell you.'

Verena looked at her, was about to say, 'Okay', when they were interrupted by Dad, shouting loudly.

'Fireworks!'

Flame squeezed her hand on Verena's arm. 'Come on,' she smiled.

'There's one more thing,' said Verena, as they walked across the field, away from the bonfire. 'What happened to the ghost?'

Flame laughed. 'Oh, she's left. She's not unhappy any more.'

'I know you saw her around me that night. I could see her, clear as day.'

'Yes, I know.'

Then Verena said, 'Daddy and I called Mummy this afternoon.'

'That's wonderful! I'm sure she'll be home soon.'

'Then Grandma can go away and leave us in peace,' said Verena, with a grim smile.

They stopped in front of the rope Dad had set up for the fireworks display. Everyone crowded around, and for the next half-hour they were regaled by the display. Huge, roaring rockets, colourful starbursts, whizzing Catherine Wheels and spiders of bright white light lit up the sky over the Big Field.

Dad and Charles worked together to keep the display going from one firework to the next.

The Sprite family and their guests looked up with rapt faces.

'Beautiful!' cried Mum.

'Lovely!' exclaimed Harry.

'Fantastic!' shouted Marina.

As the fireworks lit up the sky, the Sprite Sisters came together, as if drawn by an invisible force. Flame, Marina, Ash and Ariel stood close, their faces shining with enjoyment. And, in the middle of the little group, stood Verena Glass, her eyes bright and happy.

As the last firework exploded in a burst of blue light, Ariel whispered, 'Magic.'

SPECIAL THANKS

Thank you to all the Piccadilly Press team for their skill, effort and enthusiasm, especially Brenda Gardner, Mary Byrne, Margot Edwards, Vivien Tesseras, Melissa Hyder and Victoria Lee. Particular thanks to my whizz editor, Anne Clark, for her sharp eyes and sound judgment. Also to Chris Winn for bringing the Sprite world to life in his drawing and to Anna Gould and Simon Davis for their fourth striking cover.

Thank you to Veronique Baxter and Laura West at David Higham Associates.

Thank you to Bob Davey for his advice on boreholes and engineering.

Thank you to my parents, Alan & Janet Ebbage, and to my friends – especially Liz Dittner, Carol Fairhurst, Charlotte & Henry Crawley, James & Carolyn Spencer Ashworth, Sally & Teddy Maufe, Caroline Holland and Deborah Shannon – for their kindness and support.

Thank you to Rosie, Alex & Hils for their boundless enthusiasm. Lastly, Sprite Sister fans – great big thanks to you all! Keep Spriting!

FIND OUT MORE ABOUT THE SPRITE SISTERS AND CONTACT THE AUTHOR:

WWW.SHERIDANWINN.COM